THE BANISHED CHILD

A Study in Tonga Oral Literature

Clement Abiaziem Okafor

To my father, Ngoli,

Who gave his life

That my life might thrive

The Banished Child:
  A Study in Tonga Oral Literature

© C.A. Okafor 1983

First published in 1983 by The Folklore Society,
c/o University College London, Gower Street,
London WC1E 6BT.

Printed in Great Britain by Rowland Phototypesetting

British Library Cataloguing in Publication Data

Okafor, C.A.
  The banished child.——(Mistletoe series; 16)
  1. Folk literature, Tonga——History and
  criticism
  I. Title   II. Series
  896'.39   PL 8010

  ISBN 0-903515-06-7

PREFACE

The aim of this book is, firstly, to define the qualities that make the Tonga tradition of cante-fable worthy of being considered as literature. Secondly, it is to isolate and describe the themes in the tradition, as represented by a sample of one hundred typical tales. These narratives are selected from a collection which I have recorded in four areas - Monze, Mwanachingwala, Chona, and Mansa - which together epitomize Tonga society.

Since it is assumed that every narrative in the tradition is defined by the habits of thematic composition witnessed in all other performances, a detailed examination of any one of these tales is a valid starting point in a study of the cante-fable tradition as a whole. The tale of the Banished Child - as performed by Scholastica Mutinta in narrative No.7 of the collection - is chosen as the starting point in this investigation.

The method used here is to isolate the themes present in narrative No.7 as well as in the six other multiforms of the tale in the sample. A description of the themes, as manifested in the entire tradition which is represented by the sample of cante-fables, then follows. This procedure is in keeping with the listening habits of a traditional audience, which normally visualizes several multiforms of a given theme known to them, rather than a specific form presented in a particular narrative.

Further examination of narrative No.7 reveals that there are two main levels of compositional organization in the typical Tonga cante-fable: the thematic, and the linear levels of organization. In addition, both levels of compositional organization are later shown to be circumscribed by the tradition; thus, validating the assumption made at the beginning of this study: that every narrative is defined by the habits of composition witnessed in all other performances in the entire cante-fable tradition.

Apart from Chapter II, which is a later addition, and Chapters III, IV, V and VI, which have been reorganized, this book is essentially the thesis that I submitted in April 1975 in partial fulfilment of the requirements for the degree of Doctor of Philosophy at Harvard University, Cambridge, Massachusetts.

I am indebted to the countless conteurs of Tonga tradition who performed patiently for me and graciously answered even my most embarrassing queries. Special thanks go to Chief Monze, Chief Chona, and Chief Mwanachingwala for their fatherly interest in my fieldwork, and to the University of Zambia for sponsoring the research project.

I am particularly indebted to Professor Albert Lord, Chairman of my Committee; to Professor Kenneth Dike, my mentor and guardian; and to Professor David Bynum, my thesis adviser and friend. I am happy to have this opportunity to express my deep gratitude to them for years of inspiring guidance and never-failing help.

I am also indebted to Hilda Ellis Davidson, Editor of the Mistletoe Series, for her encouragement and advice as to how to transform what was previously a thesis into the present book, and to Stewart Sanderson, who read the manuscript and made a number of helpful suggestions.

Finally, I should like to express my warm gratitude to my wife, Rose. She was at my side throughout the writing of the thesis and the years of preparation of this book. Without her constant encouragement and love this endeavour would certainly not have seen the light of day.

C. A. O.

Department of English,
University of Nigeria, Nsukka,
October, 1978.

CONTENTS

CHAPTER I

THE PEOPLE AND THEIR ORAL TRADITION

The Land and Its People

The Tonga of Southern Zambia are a Bantu-speaking people. Culturally and linguistically they are related to the Lenje who live to the north and to the Ila who live to the west. The Tonga together with the Ila and the Lenje constitute the *Bantu Botatwe* Central African people who speak a common language.

The Tonga inhabit an area that is bounded to the north by the Kafue River and to the south by the Zambezi River. Their territory is divided into two natural zones: the Batoka plateau and the Zambezi valley. Each zone has a different climate; the plateau is cool most of the year, receives adequate rainfall and is therefore good for agriculture, while the valley is hot almost all year round - unbearably so particularly in October. In addition, the valley receives very scanty rainfall and is thus arid despite its proximity to the Zambezi River.

Since the beginning of the colonial era, the territory has been divided from north to south by a railway track, known as the line of rail, with a four-mile stretch of land on either side reserved exclusively for non-African settlement. With Zambia's attainment of political independence, many alien farmers are selling out to Zambian farmers; hence this artificial demarcation may disappear eventually. At the present time, however, it is a significant landmark.

The Tonga have three distinct seasons. Barring yearly variations, the rainy season, *meensa*, begins in November and continues till March; the cold, dry season, *impeyo*, lasts from April till August; and the hot and dry season, *nkasalo*, arrives in September and lasts till the beginning of the rains in November. Planting - with maize as the principal crop - usually begins with the coming of the first rains and the harvesting of the crops begins in the cold, dry season. When the harvesting is over, the rest of the

1

cold season is a period of relaxation and leisure.
More important for the present investigation, it is
the ideal season when cante-fables and various genres
of oral literature are performed.

Although crop-production is a very important agricultural activity in Tonga society, it is not the
only one; the Tonga are also pastoralists, and the
raising of cattle is another important occupation
among them.

Not much is known about the origins of the Tonga,
but recent archaeological evidence suggests that they
have inhabited their present territory from at least
300 AD[1]. This makes them if not the earliest,
certainly one of the very earliest ethnic groups in
modern Zambia to settle in the country.

Tonga society is an egalitarian one and the people
have a degree of independence from kinship ties that
is unusual for a rural African community. A villager
here is free to choose whether to live with his patri-
lineal kinsmen or with his matrilineal ones; he is
equally at liberty to settle among total strangers.

The society differs from some of its neighbours -
the Lozi to the southwest and the Ndebele to the
south - which have traditionally had strong monarch-
ies endowed with considerably centralized authority.
On the contrary, Tonga society has traditionally comprised numerous largely independent villages with
little centralized authority. Within each Tonga
village the authority of the village chief over the
residents of the village is minimal; traditionally,
he was no more than a respected first among equals.
In the colonial era, however, the alien administration grouped these chiefs into a hierarchy with Chief
Monze as the Paramount Chief and endowed the chiefs
with more powers than they wielded traditionally.
Although this hierarchy has survived into the post-
colonial era, it has not significantly affected the
traditional relationships between a villager and his
chief.

Unlike the situation found in many African societies, the village is not the focus of an ordinary
Tonga's life. On the contrary, it is the matrilineal
group which performs that function. In theory the
matrilineal group comprises everyone who shares a

2

common ancestress, but in practice it usually in-
cludes only those members of the matrilineage who
live near enough to one another to be able to fulfil
reciprocal obligations. The matrilineage is certainly the most stable institution and is the func-
tional base on which the society stands. As Colson
rightly pointed out: 'It is the matrilineal group,
and not the clan,' and not the village for that
matter, 'which acts in inheritance, which provides
and shares bride wealth, which accepts responsibility
for its members.'[2] The matrilineage is pivotal in
the life of the society because the inheritance
involved here is not merely of property and wife but
of the spirits of all dead kinsmen as well.

Theoretically, the matrilineage is undifferentiated
and real brothers and sisters are supposed not to
have a greater claim to inheritance than other members of the group. In present-day practice, however,
there is a tendency for the opposite to happen.

The Nature of the Cante-Fable Tradition

The cante-fables which are the basis of this study
were collected between 1969 and 1971 in four major
areas - Monze, Mwanachingwala, Chona, and Mansa -
after a preliminary study carried out earlier in
Ufwenuka. These four areas were selected for intensive field-work largely because together they
epitomize Tonga society. In the first place Monze
and Mwanachingwala are located to the west of the
line of rail, while Chona and Mansa lie to the east
of it. Again some of the villages, particularly in
Monze, are quite close to the urban centre of Monze,
while those in Mwanachingwala are far from any such
urban centres. By recording in such places I tried
to ensure that my collection of tales included cante-
fables narrated by some Tonga whose lives had not
been affected significantly by the alien culture of
the urban areas, while at the same time including
some narrated by the Tonga who have had to accommo-
date some elements of European culture in their
everyday lives. Finally, these four areas were
selected for intensive field-work because Elizabeth

Colson conducted some intensive studies in them earlier. By working in the same areas as Colson did, I have been able to use her numerous works as a supplement to my own field observation.

The following description of the Tonga cante-fable tradition is based primarily on the responses of the story-tellers to a questionnaire administered immediately after each performance, and also on my own observation during the field-work.

In keeping with the generally egalitarian nature of Tonga society, where there are hardly any secret societies or organizations with exclusive membership, all the cante-fables in the tradition belong to the community as a whole; all the story-tellers interviewed asserted without exception that none of the cante-fables in the tradition belonged exclusively to any clan or groups of individuals. Furthermore, the informants stated that everyone in the society who so desired might learn and narrate whichever cante-fable he pleased. Hence, the ability to narrate cante-fables in this tradition is restricted neither on the basis of sex nor on the basis of age, since men and women, boys and girls can and often do narrate them. As one would expect, mature men and women are generally better at this than very young boys and girls, although some youngsters - especially those whose parents are excellent story-tellers - may be as good as the elderly narrators.

The ideal time of day for such narratives is at night, after supper. Some informants said that it was taboo to narrate such stories in day-time and stated categorically that they would never do this. Most informants, however, were more flexible; they admitted that although night-time was the ideal time, they would readily narrate such tales in day-time if importuned to do so. In fact, some of the cante-fables in my collection were narrated in day-time.

The ideal season for narrating cante-fables is the cold, dry season after the harvest. Again the informants were divided on this issue; the more rigid ones said that they would not narrate a cante-fable during any other season, but the more flexible ones said that if someone asked them to do so they would narrate these tales during any season of the year, provided it did not interfere with their farm-work. Thus it is clear that the narrative sessions generally take place at night during the cold, dry season, especially during the period of rest following the harvest - and for a good reason too.

The traditional explanation as to why the narrative sessions do not take place in day-time was because a whirlwind would carry away those who broke the taboo. A corresponding explanation as to why the narrative sessions did not take place during the planting season was because the people were afraid that doing so would harm the corn growing in the fields. When questioned further, however, most informants admitted that they did not believe that such disasters would indeed occur. Evidently these traditional explanations were no more than convenient explanations for the way the society conducted its affairs, and one has to look elsewhere for a more convincing reason.

A plausible explanation deduced by the present investigator from his field-experience in the area is that such regulations pertaining to the appropriate time and season for narrating cante-fables is a rational method by which the society eliminates the kind of behaviour that is considered inimical to its economic survival. Tonga society is, after all, a rural and agricultural community of subsistence farmers, for whom food-production is a very important occupation. If the population were to narrate cante-fables in day-time during the farming season, this would undoubtedly disrupt the production of food, which in turn would produce the disastrous famines lamented so often in Tonga cante-fables. Therefore, by shrouding the pragmatic need for food-production in a quasi-religious taboo, the society is actually using psychological and religious sanctions to enforce its prohibition of story-telling during the periods of the year when it considers that the villagers should give their undivided attention to agriculture.

Every story-teller was asked after each performance whether the cante-fable he had just performed had a title. Most said no, but a few said yes; some mentioned titles by which they remembered the tales. These often turned out to be some incapsulation of the central idea of the tale, as they perceived it, or some catch-words in the accompanying song. Asked if they would be able to narrate the preceding tale when they heard such catch-words, most people in the audience protested that they could not. One may therefore conclude that although there are idiosyncratic devices which some individuals use in order to recall some tales, the cante-fables in this tradition do not have generally-accepted titles.

The events narrated in the cante-fables are generally believed to have happened. Most of the tellers and the audiences interviewed believed that the incidents must have happened in some distant past, although they all agreed that the fantastic events, such as a human being rescuing his or her relative from the land of the dead or events like animals transforming themselves into human beings and vice versa, could not happen at the present time.

The composition of the audience varied from one performance to another. At some narrative sessions the audience comprised a man, his wife and their dependent children who happened to live with them at the time. At other sessions, especially those that took place at the home of a chief or a village-head, the audiences were considerably larger. Fifteen men, twenty-three women, ten boys and eight girls comprised the audience at one such session that took place in Chief Mwanachingwala's home. These large audiences were unusual, however; narrative sessions were usually private rather than social affairs for the members of one family and their guests.

The narrative sessions were ordinarily informal and even in the ones that involved a large audience and the presence of a chief, people drifted in and out at will, thereby often distracting the audience and occasionally the story-teller himself. The story-teller's ability to retain the attention of his audience therefore depended to a large extent on his narrative skill. A good narrator could capture and retain his audience's attention to the extent that it would not notice the distractions. On the other hand, a mediocre narrator was apt to lose the attention of his audience and might even have to halt his narrative for a while, especially during the entrance or exit of a very important member of the community.

The audiences at these narrative sessions were usually participatory ones, and often played vital roles during the narrative sessions themselves. The audiences constantly answered *'Kalungutu'* or *'Kalangati'* (We are listening) after each major cadence in the narrative. In addition, the audience functioned as the chorus during the singing of the numerous songs in the various narratives. Tonga audiences were essentially critical audiences, for they often aided young story-tellers who seemed to have some difficulties in their composition; they encouraged talented narrators by applauding at the appropriate moments, but they also made uncomplimentary comments if a story-teller did not perform as well as was expected of him.

Narrators frequently used various dramatic devices like mimicry, pantomime and dance to enliven their performances. Often it was the talented story-tellers who used these devices with most dramatic effect. One such narrator was Scholastica Mutinta - narrator of my narrative No.7 - who re-enacted for her audience all the actions of the characters in her narratives. In No.7, for instance, she used her hands to demonstrate how the mother of the twin boys improvised the bark of a tree to serve as a blanket for her banished children. She appropriately demonstrated the wrestling contest between the twins in the narrative and their foster-parent. In addition, she used a change of voice to portray the dialogue between the mother and the twin sons whom she had imagined were lost. She crouched down in order to depict the jealous husband and his colleagues who lay in ambush while his unsuspecting wife came by singing. Indeed only a film would adequately convey the level of dramatization employed by her and other talented story-tellers in the tradition.

Unlike the *griots* in the Sahel region of West Africa, whom some have said are professionals, nobody made a living from narrating these tales. There was also no formal association of story-tellers, and since every member of the society who so desired could narrate the cante-fables, the ability to do so did not detract from one's social status. If anything, it temporarily enhanced a talented story-teller's standing in society - if only for the duration of the performance - because he was ordinarily the focus of his audience's attention, and if he performed well his audiences praised him and held him in high esteem. There was no evidence to suggest, however, that the ability to perform cante-fables well conferred high status on the narrators outside a narrative situation.

The process of transmission in the tradition was a very informal one. A formal teacher-novice situation did not exist here, neither was there a formal apprenticeship; hence, the learning process did not call for the performance of initiatory rituals before, during or after the period of apprenticeship.

In this tradition, the student might choose his teacher as often as the teacher chose his student. But often choice was not a factor; a youngster usually learnt his first few stories from the best story-teller in the family, who might be his father, mother, paternal or maternal grand-parent, depending on whether the youngster grew up in the home of his grand-parents or at the home of his own parents. The teacher might even be an elder herdsboy with whom the youngster shared the herding of the village cattle.

The art of story-telling seemed to be on the decline, for in many families people did not gather around the fireplace during the cold winter months any more to listen to cante-fables as they used to do in the past. This was attributable to the prohibition imposed by the early Christian missionaries on such narratives, on the mistaken assumption that they were aspects of 'Devil-worship'. Since the missionaries had been very active in the territory for more than half a century, the prohibition has begun to affect the habits of even non-Christian Tonga people, and because people did not gather often to narrate cante-fables, they have slowly lost their narrative skill. The result is that at the present time many people, particularly Christians between twenty-five and forty years old, confess that they cannot narrate any tale at all. Even when these tried, they were often unable to narrate a cante-fable coherently. Those Tonga who did not break completely with the tradition still composed complex and entertaining tales.

Most of the story-tellers interviewed were convinced that their narrative tradition had declined considerably since the advent of the missionaries in their territory, and they gave the impression that in the past every normal adult could narrate at least a few tales reasonably well. It is possible that the informants have painted an exaggerated picture of the past, but this investigator found some evidence which suggested that the tradition was actually declining. Those who still composed complex and entertaining stories had a limited repertoire, and even the very talented story-teller, Scholastica Mutinta, could narrate only three cante-fables. Undoubtedly the current tradition dates back to many generations, but it could not have survived for so long if the repertoire of its narrators had always been as limited as it was during my field-work.

With the advent of national independence and the repudiation of many of the notions engendered by alien missionaries, the government of Zambia is attempting to revive the narrative tradition by incorporating it into the school curriculum. In Zambia, however - as in many other African countries - most of those who succeed in school eventually live in the urban areas, which are not ideal settings in which a cante-fable tradition can flourish. Consequently the decline in Tonga cante-fable tradition may well be irreversible.

The one hundred tales used in this study represent a wide cross-section of the entire tradition. They were selected in such a way as to ensure that all the four major areas of intensive recording and all the categories of people who traditionally narrated cante-fables were represented. Thus some tales in the sample were narrated by old men or women, some by young boys or girls, and some by middle-aged men and women. Once a narrator was selected, his entire repertoire in my collection was included in the sample.

The following is a brief summary of the one hundred cante-fables that constitute my sample of the Tonga tradition. The number next to the margin is the

serial number assigned to each tale in this sample
selection. The second number is that to which the
narrative was assigned originally in my collection.

1 Narrative No.1: a Tonga rendering of the
Cinderella story, which is an import from the
European narrative tradition, since the name of its
principal character - Sindela - is not found elsewhere in Tonga tradition. This tale, narrated by an
agricultural officer, is exceptional because the
story-teller had learnt it from a foreign anthology.
It merits inclusion in the sample, however, because
it illustrates what happens to a tale when it is
transplanted from one culture to another. In this
Tonga rendering, Sindela is born into a polygamous
family. When Sindela's mother dies, the mother's co-
wife begins to maltreat Sindela and forces her to
minister to her own children. One day, Sindela's
dead mother, assuming the guise of a soul-bird,
appears to Sindela, and equips her with beautiful
clothes which enable her to attract the attention of
a prince. He eventually marries her and saves her
from the misery in her home.

2 Narrative No.2: how a Hare dupes a Lion, which is
about to kill a *Kudu* (antelope). In this story as
well as in many others in the tradition, the Hare is
portrayed as a trickster. He is usually cleverer
than most of the other animals and he constantly
dupes and exploits them at will. In this story, the
Lion, having previously fed Kudu's offspring to its
own cub, now wants to eat the Kudu herself. While
the terrified Kudu pleads with the Lion to no avail,
Hare, the trickster passes by and asks the Lion to
help him lift a heavy stone slab. The gullible Lion
releases his captive in order to lift the slab. By
distracting the Lion in this way, the Hare makes it
possible for the Kudu to escape.

3 Narrative No.3: this describes the unhappy friendship between Hare, the trickster, and a Lion. The
two friends devise a plan, which enables them to kill
other animals for food. Eventually, however, the
Hare ensnares and wilfully kills the Lion too.

10

4 Narrative No.4: this tells of the exploits of a
Hare who, impersonating a Lion, deceives some Hyenas
into believing that he is indeed the Lion. The
gullible Hyenas entertain the Hare lavishly until
eventually they find out that the Hare is not the
King of the animals as they thought. Furious, the
Hyenas pursue the Hare, intending to kill him, but
the crafty Hare eludes them.

5 Narrative No.5: an account of the exploits of
Hare's wife. It shows how a pregnant Hare ensnares a
nursing Hyena, a Lioness, and a Sow, and milks them
against their will. The female Hare later drinks the
milk.

6 Narrative No.6: this comprises two stories which
do not always occur together in the tradition. The
first portrays the banishment of an unwanted child
and its mother, while the second is the tale of a
monster bird that swallows human beings. A young
man, needing many children to herd his cattle, banishes his wife who has only one living child. On her
way home, the banished woman takes her only child
with her, leaving her husband with his favourite wife
and her five children. One day, however, the favourite wife, defying all wise counsel, foolishly goes
into a forest in search of her husband who is hunting
wild animals. There a monster-bird waylays her and
gobbles up all her five children one after the other.

7 Narrative No.7: an account of twin brothers who
are banished from home. Wanting the twins to die,
their father orders them to be thrown away, but their
mother instead hides them in a cave in a nearby
forest. While the twins are in the forest, a benevolent spirit adopts them and provides them with all
the good things of life. Hence the banishment which
was to have killed them paradoxically brings them
great fortune.

8 Narrative No.8: a humorous account of how a Hare
deceives his friend into throwing his food into a
stream. Later, on arriving with the same friend at
the home of the Hare's kinsmen, the Hare kills their

hosts' goat and smears its blood on his unsuspecting
friend, making it appear that the friend has killed
the animal. Eventually the owners of the goat find
out who really killed it, but as is usual in such
tales, the Hare escapes unscathed.

9 Narrative No.11: this portrays an old woman who
has no child of her own. She regularly stores blood
from her leachings in a pot. After a while the blood
turns itself into a girl who is so beautiful that
jealous neighbours kidnap her. Eventually, the old
woman pulls off the hair which sustains the girl's
life and thereby transforms her into waste blood once
more.

10 Narrative No.13: a story about three friends who
set out to hunt. Because one, Moonga, has a dog, he
is able to kill game animals while his friends cannot.
Moonga's friends become jealous and kill him, but his
dog escapes and exposes the murderers. Consequently
Moonga's companions are executed when they return to
the village.

11 Narrative No.14: this depicts an old woman who,
pretending to be ill, escapes having to work, and
stays at home, while her kinsmen work hard on the
farm. But she does not stay in bed as a sick person
should, and instead dances to the music which a dog
plays for her. Ultimately her kinsmen discover what
has been happening and kill her.

12 Narrative No.15: this is about a group of girls
who, setting out from home to be tatooed, arrive at
the home of a Guinea-fowl. One of the girls enters
so that the Guinea-fowl may tatoo her, but her companions seek the services of some-one else. When the
girls all return home, the other girls notice that
the tatoo on their companion who sought the services
of the Guinea-fowl is far more beautiful than theirs.
So the other girls, deciding to be tatooed again, set
out this time for the home of the Guinea-fowl. But
they do not achieve their objective; they lose their
way and finally meet an old woman who invites them to
spend the night at her home. Later the old woman

invites some Lions to eat her guests, but the girls
manage to escape and the Lions turn on the old woman
and devour her.

13 Narrative No.16: an account of a woman who is
supposed to feed a Cock in return for the protection
it offers her. After some time she begins to neglect
feeding the Cock and, when the bird is too weak to
shield her, a monster, Seezimwe, overpowers and
swallows the negligent woman. Her relatives later
kill the monster and rescue the woman.

14 Narrative No.17: a story of how an unlikely com-
petitor wins the hand of a shy and handsome young
man, Tembo, who lives in a river. All the beautiful
girls in the neighbourhood try without success to
become Tembo's bride, but the one he finally accepts
is the ugliest girl in the area.

15 Narrative No.18: a multiform of narrative No.7.
It is narrated by the mother of the conteuse of narrative No.7, and is an account of the twin boys who
are banished by their own father. But the banishment
brings the twins good fortune rather than the death
their father had hoped for them.

16 Narrative No.19: a multiform of narrative No.11,
telling of a young man, Sinyawi Nyawi, who marries an
unnatural bride. His wife is a piece of wood
fashioned into the likeness of a human being and
later transformed into a beautiful woman. Some people become so jealous of the pretty wife that they
kidnap her. Eventually Sinyawi Nyawi finds her and
pulls off the feather that sustains her life. By so
doing, he turns not only his wife but the entire
village of her abductors into trees.

17 Narrative No.20: the story of an *enfant terrible*
who sets out on a bride-quest when he is merely one
day old. He proves his magical powers by eating
poisoned food, bathing in water that kills anyone it
touches, and climbing a magical palm-tree, thus pas-
sing tests which have already claimed the lives of
five earlier suitors. Finally he marries the much-

sought-after girl and takes her back to his own home.

18 Narrative No.21: the story of a girl whose
father banishes her because he wants only boys to be
born into his household. The girl's mother hides her
in a forest where an old woman rears her until she is
finally accepted and taken back by her father. This
is a multi-form of narratives 7 and 18.

19 Narrative No.22: the account of a race between a
Tortoise and a Hare. Confident that he will out-
distance the slow Tortoise, the nimble Hare challenges the Tortoise to compete against him. The
Tortoise readily accepts the challenge and wins the
contest in the end by playing tricks on the Hare.
Although multiforms of the tale exist in Aesop's
Fables, it is not an import from the European tradition. On the contrary, the story, current also in
the Igbo tradition, is an Old World tale.

20 Narrative No.23: this depicts an old woman who
persuades her only son to marry so that his new wife
will care for her in her old age. After a short
while, the new wife decides not to care for her
mother-in-law any more, and the old lady procures a
talisman which enables her to lure the daughter-in-
law into a forest. There she abandons the unsuspecting young woman on a tree-top.

21 Narrative No.24: a tale about a group of girls
who set out to have their front teeth removed in
accordance with ancient Tonga tradition. All the
girls walk together except one lone girl who follows
them at a distance. The group of girls meet an old
woman in dire need of help, but they refuse to help
her. When the lonely girl meets the old woman, she
consents to assist her, and the tale ends abruptly
after this incident.
    Although the story ends without a resolution, the
narrator provided sufficient details to enable one to
conclude that this tale is a multiform of narrative
No.15, where a group of girls sets out to be tatooed.

22 Narrative No.25: a tale about a group of girls who set out to fish illegally by a dam, in a pond which is the home of evil forces. While they fish, they are attacked by a monster-bird that devours human beings. Fortunately for the girls, a younger brother of one of them saves them by putting them into a drum which flies them home to safety. This account is an amalgam of two stories which exist independently in the tradition. Multiforms of the first component - the story of a large monster-bird which devours people - exist independently in narratives 19, 29, 51, 65, and 70 and are linked to other stories in narratives 74, 81 and 116. Multiforms of the second component - the story of a young boy who saves his elder sister and her girl-companions from imminent death - exist in narratives 40 and 55.

23 Narrative No.26: a combination of two tales which do not always occur together in the tradition. The first is a story of how a wily Hare ingenuously forces a beautiful but dumb girl to speak and by so doing wins her hand in marriage. It is essentially a story of the unlikely suitor who wins a contest over his more qualified rivals. In this respect, it is a multiform of narrative No.17.

The second part of the narrative tells how Hare's jealous neighbours plot unsuccessfully to kill him and take away his beautiful wife. Hence it may be regarded, with some qualification, as a multiform of narrative No.19.

24 Narrative No.28: an account of how some jealous neighbours who, impersonating an Elephant, gain entrance into the Elephant's home. Once there, they kidnap the Elephant's beautiful wife and take her to their own home. This is a multiform of narrative No.19.

25 Narrative No.29: a story about a woman who, deciding to return to her parents after a fight with her husband, chooses to go home past a pond, despite her co-wife's warnings. She is confronted by a large monster-bird which eats all her children one at a time. Her relatives eventually kill the bird,

however, and release the woman's children. This is a multiform of narrative No.6, and the first portion of narrative No.25.

26 Narrative No.34: a story about a husband who is so selfish that he refuses to share with his wife and family the milk and corn his father-in-law has given him on behalf of his entire family. Instead, he hides the provision in a dam and secretly feeds himself whenever he is hungry. Eventually, his wife discovers his tricks, takes away the cow and maize, and returns with her son to live with her own parents.

27 Narrative No.35: a story of a married couple who decide to visit the wife's home. When they arrive and food is set before them, the wife uses a song to complain about all the bad things her husband has done to her in the past. Furious, the husband refuses to eat until his wife stops singing about their problems.

28 Narrative No.36: this describes the sufferings of a young man as he journeys through a rough and rocky countryside in search of his father's snake, which the youth earlier inadvertently released. The story ends inconclusively.

29 Narrative No.37: this is about a young man who goes to work in Johannesburg. On his return home, his father lures him into a forest. While the young man is in the top of a tree, his father transforms himself into a Lion and attempts to devour him. The young man, however, manages to summon his dog from home, and it tears the old man to pieces. Multiforms of this tale abound in the narrative tradition of the neighbouring Ila people as well as that of the Igbo of West Africa. The story is therefore a Pan-African tale.

30 Narrative No.39: this concerns another young man who goes to work in a distant land. His master rewards him by giving him a magical ring which provides him with everything he desires. Later his unfaithful wife steals the ring and uses it to build

herself and her parents a beautiful town, but eventually the young man recovers the ring. This is a multiform of narrative No.37. Again, although multiforms of this tale exist in the European tradition, it is not an import from the European tradition, since its multiform - narrative No.37 - is a Pan-African tale.

31 Narrative No.40: an account of how three girls get married to three animal suitors, and how a younger brother of one of the girls rescues them by putting them in a drum which flies them all to safety. In this respect, narrative No.40 is a multiform of the second part of narrative No.25, as has been mentioned above.

32 Narrative No.41: this is about some rats which revive themselves after hunters have killed them, dressed them, salted them and spread them out to dry in the sun. On discovering what has happened, the hunters vow neither to hunt nor to eat rats ever again.

33 Narrative No.42: a story of how an old woman arranges for several girls to be betrothed to her son, who she claims is working in a distant land. Eventually the would-be wives discover that their mother-in-law's sole purpose in keeping them in her home is to use them as farm labourers, since her son cannot marry them; he is not a complete human being but a human head. The wives therefore return to their own homes, leaving the old woman to do all her work by herself.

34 Narrative No.43: an account of how a woman journeys to the land of the dead and succeeds in recovering all her dead children. Her jealous and impetuous co-wife in her attempt to do likewise offends some of the inhabitants of the land of the dead and dies as a result.

35 Narrative No.44: this shows how a son of an elder wife in a polygamous family tries unsuccessfully to take possession of a magic wand found by his

half-brother - the son of a younger wife. The
younger boy ultimately takes the wand to his own
mother and it provides whatever good things they desire.

36 Narrative No.45: this describes the miserable
plight of a man and his family as they watch the wild
fruits, their only source of food during a devastating famine, diminish, yet there is nothing the man
can do to ameliorate the grim situation. When the
supply is totally exhausted, the man and his family
starve to death.

37 Narrative No.46: the story of a girl who is banished by her father because he does not want girls in
his household. The banished girl grows up in a forest and finally her father has a change of heart and
brings her home. This is a multiform of narratives
7, 18 and 21.

38 Narrative No.47: this is about an unnatural
child who ultimately turns into a fish. A barren old
woman who is fishing catches a fish which later transforms itself into a beautiful girl. One day when the
old woman abuses the girl, she turns herself into a
fish again and refuses to come back despite the old
woman's pleas. This is a multiform of narratives 11
and 19.

39 Narrative No.48: this is a tale of an old woman
who frightens away the prospective husbands of her
daughter by subjecting them to such tests as having
them watch while she lifts her skirt. This test is
considered particularly difficult on account of the
numerous Tonga taboos which rigidly proscribe any
kind of carnal knowledge between a prospective son-
in-law and mother-in-law. Only a group of young boys
succeed in this situation where their elders have
failed. In this respect the tale is a multiform of
narrative No.17.

40 Narrative No.49: an account of how a slave-girl
usurps the position of her mistress. In this narrative a newly-married bride who is on her first

journey to the home of her new husband loses a contest - and consequently her dress - to her slave-girl. Now garbed in the attire of a new bride, the slave-girl is mistaken for the bride, while the new bridegroom maltreats his bride as if she were the slave-girl.

41 Narrative No.50: this is about a young girl whose father is away on a long journey. Before the father sets out, he gives his daughter a dog which he instructs her to feed in return for the dog's protection. After some time, the girl neglects the dog. When it is too weak to defend the girl, some men kidnap her. This tale is a multiform of narrative No.16, and in both multiforms the negligent woman is rescued in the end.

42 Narrative No.51: this is about a foolhardy woman who sets out to visit her husband's parents. A large man-eating bird ambushes her and devours her children. In this respect, the tale is a multiform of narratives 25 and 29. Other multiforms of this story in my collection are narratives 65, 70, the first part of 74, and the second part of 81.

43 Narrative No.52: a combination of two stories that do not always occur together in the tradition. The first deals with the journey a living person makes to the land of the dead, and is a multiform of narrative 43, and the later parts of narratives 63, 79, 85 and 86. The second story in this tale deals with the acquisition of wealth through the possession of magical objects. It is a multiform of narrative No.39.

44 Narrative No.53: this shows how a small and unlikely suitor succeeds in winning a bride whom his betters are unable to procure. This story is a multiform of narratives 17, 22, 26 and 48.

45 Narrative No.54: this deals with a proposed marriage between human beings and an unnatural partner - a ghost - and is a multiform of narratives 11, 19, 47, and the first parts of 55 and 57. Here two

girls meet a handsome young man they want for a husband. When the young man declines, telling them that
he is a ghost, one of the girls agrees and returns
home. The other girl, however, stubbornly follows
the ghost to his grave. Even then she refuses to go
back until the ghost, sinking slowly into the ground,
disappears completely.

46 Narrative No.55: this consists of two stories
which do not always occur together in Tonga tradition.
The first part deals with the marriage of human
beings to unnatural partners - three animals - and is
therefore a multiform of No.54. The second deals
with a young brother who rescues his elder sister and
her companions from being devoured by their animal
partners; it is a multiform of narratives 25 and 40.

47 Narrative No.56: this is another account of the
banishment of a girl whose father does not want girls
to be born into his household. This is a multiform
of narratives 7, 18, 21, 46, and 100, and as in all
these multiforms, the father eventually welcomes his
child home again.

48 Narrative No.57: this portrays the marriage of a
human being to an unnatural bride who is a piece of
wood fashioned into human shape. Eventually, some
jealous people kidnap the bride and take her to their
own home. In this respect the story is a multiform
of narratives 11, 19 and 47. As in all the other
multiforms, the unnatural woman in this tale is
ultimately transformed back into her original element
- wood.

49 Narrative No.58: an account of how a jealous
wife in a polygamous family abducts the son of
another wife and imprisons him in a gourd. One day
the boy's parents accidentally see him leave the
gourd, play with other children in the village, and
go back into his place of captivity. Determined to
recover his son, the father hides in the playground
and captures the boy when he emerges from the gourd.
Refusing to let go of the youngster, the father succeeds in destroying the magic holding him captive.

50 Narrative No.59: a story of how a Tortoise
cheats a Baboon and how the Baboon later retaliates
on the Tortoise. The Tortoise, who invites the
Baboon to his home, insists that the Baboon wash his
palms and keep them clean before drinking. But
Tortoise, the trickster, has burnt a patch of grass
outside his house; thus the Baboon's hands are always
soiled before he enters the Tortoise's home. After
washing and soiling his hands a couple of times, the
Baboon gives up and meekly watches his host drink all
the wine by himself. Some time later, the Baboon
invites the Tortoise to his home. By insisting that
the Tortoise climb into the Baboon's home in the
treetop, the Baboon ensures that his guest does not
share in the meal. This is a Pan-African tale because its multiforms are found in the cante-fable
tradition of the Igbo of West Africa.

51 Narrative No.60: this shows how a jealous young
man kills his younger brother because the youngster
is more successful than he. In this respect, this
tale is a multiform of narratives 13 and 92, and as
in these multiforms the murderer is eventually
exposed and executed for his crime.

52 Narrative No.61: this is about a beautiful bride
who leaves her husband's bed every night, turns herself into an animal, and grazes in the bush nearby.
When her husband finally sees her grazing in her
animal form, the woman flees into the bush and returns no more.

53 Narrative No.62: this is about children who
regularly go into a nearby forest in order to collect
wild fruit. On each occasion an old woman in a tree-
top begs them not to exhaust the fruits which she
says are her only means of sustenance. When the
youngsters take their elders to the forest, they are
unable to see the woman who is quite visible to the
youngsters. The tale ends without resolution; but
the situation in which an elder and a younger person
go into a forest in order to collect some wild fruit
is reminiscent of narrative No.23.

54 Narrative No.63: an account of how strenuous and
unfamiliar tasks destroy a new bride. Each time
Mwisya, the new bride, pounds peanuts she sinks a
little further into the earth. Finally, she is completely swallowed by the earth. When this happens,
everyone including her parents tries without success
to rescue her. Only Mwisya's youngest sister manages
to bring her back to life.

55 Narrative No.64: the story of a lazy girl who
foolishly allows the sun to escape. The lazy girl
recruits her friends to do her work; in return she
entertains them by allowing them to play with her
father's most-prized possession - the sun. Unfortunately the sun escapes and instals itself in the sky.
Chagrined, the girl's father flogs her.

56 Narrative No.65: this is about a foolhardy wife
who decides to leave her husband and return to her
parents' home. Disregarding the wise and friendly
advice of her co-wife, she chooses to take a dangerous path which is haunted by a monster-bird. The
bird confronts and kills her before she can get the
help of her kinsmen. The tale is a multiform of
narrative No.6.

57 Narrative No.66B: this is about a pregnant woman
who is abandoned in a tree-top by her husband. Crav-
ing figs, the woman constantly nags her husband until
he finally takes her to a forest where both of them
climb a fig tree. The woman is so greedy, however,
that she does not let her husband eat any of the
fruit, and so the husband abandons her in the tree-
top. In this respect the tale is a multiform of
narratives 23, 37 and 96.

58 Narrative No. 68A: this portrays a woman who maltreats the daughter of her dead co-wife. The dead
woman, however, comes to the aid of her living offspring. This tale is therefore a multiform of the
first part of narratives 1 and 79.

59 Narrative No.69: this depicts a man who is so
selfish that he will not share his resources - some

wild fruits - with his family during a famine.
Eventually, his wife discovers the place where he
hides the fruits. In retaliation, she takes all the
fruits for herself and her children. The tale is a
multiform of narrative No.34.

60 Narrative No.70: this is about a young boy who
guards his father's distant farm against marauders.
Instead of driving away the predators, however, the
youngster is attacked by a large, menacing bird which
continually devours his food. When the young boy
finally returns home emaciated, his people set out
with him for the farm. They set a trap for the bird
and succeed in killing it.

61 Narrative No.71: a multiform of narrative No.41,
an account of how some rats revive themselves after
hunters have killed, salted and dried them in the sun.
When the hunters discover what has been happening,
they vow never again to hunt or eat rats.

62 Narrative No.73: this concerns a hunter's dis-
obedient wife. Before the hunter leaves home, he
instructs her to cook good food for his hunting dog.
The wife obeys the instruction for some time, but
rebels after a while and gives the dog unpalatable
food. Angered by this shabby treatment, the dog
bites off one of the woman's breasts and runs away to
its original home. This tale is a multiform of narratives 16 and 50, in that all three deal with a
woman's neglect of the pet which she is instructed to
care for.

63 Narrative No.74: the story about a man who
chooses to farm a nearby burial ground. A large bird
which lives there frustrates his efforts by reviving
every shrub the farmer cuts down. Each time the man
catches the bird and tries to kill it, the bird revives itself. In the end, the farmer gives up his
attempt to farm the graveyard. The tale is a multiform of narratives 41 and 71.

64 Narrative No.75: an account of an old woman who
collects blood from her leachings. After a while,

23

the blood transforms itself into a girl who is so beautiful that certain men abduct her. The old woman manages to discover the girl's whereabouts and bring her back home, but the men kidnap her again. Finally the old woman transforms the girl into her former constituent - blood. The tale is thus a multiform of narratives 11, 19, 47 and 57.

65 <u>Narrative No.76</u>: an account of the marriage of two human brides to two animals masquerading as human beings. It tells how the younger brother of one of the brides rescues the brides from being eaten by their husbands. The tale is a multiform of narratives 25 and 40.

66 <u>Narrative No.77</u>: this is about a lazy man, Sikulu Siyamba, who plays his drum while others toil on their farms. During the harvesting season he tries to steal other people's crops, but is caught in the act and the crops taken away from him.

67 <u>Narrative No.78</u>: this is about two close friends whom certain jealous neighbours try unsuccessfully to set against one another. Their friendship is so strong, however, that it survives, and is even strengthened by their neighbours' interference.

68 <u>Narrative No.79</u>: this shows how a dead mother assists her living daughter who is being maltreated by the dead woman's co-wife. The father of the maltreated girl finally recovers his formerly dead wife alive from the river, and sacrifices a cow to the river to show his gratitude. The tale is a multiform of narratives 1 and 68A.

69 <u>Narrative No.80</u>: this shows how an old witch who lives in the forest eats a young mother's child. When the bereaved mother reports the incident to her husband, the man sets a trap for the old woman by inviting her to a feast in his house. In this way, he is able to lure her to his home and kill her. This is a multiform of narrative No.97.

70 <u>Narrative No.81</u>: this is a combination of two

stories which do not always go together. The first
is that of animals who procure human brides, a multiform of which occurs in narratives 25, 40, and 76.
The second is that of a large monster-bird which
preys on human beings, multiforms of which are found
in narratives 29, 51 and 74.

71 Narrative No.82: this portrays how a young boy
journeys to a distant a stony country in order to
bring home a snake which cures his elder kinsman of a
serious illness. It is a multiform of narrative
No.36, since both narratives deal with journeys whose
objective is the procurement of a treasured snake.

72 Narrative No.83: a story about a wayward girl
who refuses to be married. Instead she spends all
her time carousing in a nearby city and comes home
late every night. One night a Lion impersonates her
and is thus admitted to the girl's home, where it
devours the girl's parents. When the girl returns
home later that night, the Lion eats her too.

73 Narrative No.84: an account of how a Hare succeeds in drawing water from a well dug by other animals. The Hare refused to join in digging the well,
and the owners station guards to see he draws no
water, but on each occasion the Hare deceives the
guard and uses the well. He is eventually caught,
but he manages to escape the punishment meted out to
him.

74 Narrative No.85: this tells how a Hare deceives
a Fox into killing his mother. The Fox, however,
revives her when he takes her to the land of the dead.
When the jealous Hare kills his own mother and tries
to revive her, he fails. This tale is a multiform of
narrative 43 and the first part of narrative 52.

75 Narrative No. 86: a multiform of narrative No.85.
It is a story of how a Hare goads a Fox into killing
his mother and how the Fox succeeds in reviving her.
When the Tortoise tries to do likewise, he fails.

76 Narrative No.87: this shows how a girl who

25

steals the fruit that belong collectively to herself
and her friends is punished. Because none of the
girls is willing to admit that she has stolen the
fruit, all have to go to a nearby river so that the
oracle of the river can find out the guilty one.
Predictably, the river swallows the culprit.

77 Narrative No.88: this shows how two handicapped
friends - one lame and the other blind - cure one
another. First the lame man mischievously feeds his
friend a toad while he himself consumes the nutri-
tious meat that belongs to both of them. But the
toad paradoxically cures the blind man, and when he
sees what his lame friend made him eat, he is so
infuriated that he beats the lame man mercilessly.
Unexpectedly this cures the lame man.

78 Narrative No.89: an account of how an unnatural
bride fashioned out of wood is kidnapped by jealous
neighbours and is later transformed back into wood by
her own husband. It is a multiform of narratives 11,
19, 47, 57 and 75.

79 Narrative No.90: this portrays a human bride who
eventually transforms herself into an animal. In
this story, the male head of a household is an alco-
holic, and not only often neglects to care for his
family but frequently fights with his wife. When the
wife cannot bear the situation any more she transforms herself into a zebra. This tale is a multiform
of narratives 11, 19, 47, 54, 55, 57, 75, 89 and
especially 61.

80 Narrative No.92: a story about certain friends
who set out to buy some hoes from a distant land.
Because one of them is more successful than the rest,
the others become jealous and kill him. The murdered person turns himself into a soul-bird and
exposes his companions when they return home. As a
result, the murderers are put to death. This is a
multiform of narratives 13 and 60.

81 Narrative No.93: this shows a father's attempts
to bring back his daughter who has eloped and is

living with her husband without the father's consent.
Of all the male kinsmen delegated to bring the girl
home, only the young boys succeed. In this respect,
the tale is a multiform of narratives 11, 19, 47, 57,
75 and 89.

82 Narrative No.94: an account of how a Frog burns
her husband, a Chameleon, to death. The Chameleon
asks his wife to set fire to a nearby patch of grass.
When the fire begins to burn, each of them tries to
leap over it. The Frog succeeds in leaping over the
flames, but the Chameleon falls into the fire and
dies.

83 Narrative No.95: this is about a man who marries
a beautiful bride who turns out to be a cannibal.
The husband soon learns to relish human flesh too,
and not long afterwards the newly-married couple
devour both their families.

84 Narrative No.96: this tells how a nagging wife
compels her husband to take her to a nearby forest to
collect wild fruit. When the woman and her husband
climb a fig tree to collect the fruit, the woman
refuses to let her husband eat any. The man abandons
his wife at the top of the tree and returns home.
This is a multiform of narratives 23, 37 and 66B.

85 Narrative No.97: an account of how an old witch
who lives in a forest eats a young mother's baby.
When the bereaved mother informs her husband of what
has befallen their child, the husband sets a trap for
the old woman by inviting her to his home. This
enables him to kill the old witch and avenge the
death of his child. This tale is a multiform of
narrative No.80.

86 Narrative No.98: a story about a female Frog
which cheats a female Chameleon out of the reward due
to her for working hard on the farm. In the end the
Frog is exposed and punished for being lazy.

87 Narrative No.99: a multiform of narratives 41
and 71, an account of how some rats resuscitate

27

themselves after hunters have killed them and dried
them in the sun.

88 Narrative No.100: this portrays a girl who is
banished because her father wants only boys in his
household. It is a multiform of narratives 7, 18, 21,
46 and 46, and as is the case in all these multiforms,
the banished child is brought home in the end by the
father who banished it.

89 Narrative No.102: an account of a pregnant woman
who wants her husband to give her eggs to eat. Reluctantly, the husband goes into a forest, climbs a tree
and steals a wild bird's egg for his wife. After
repeated trips, the bird finally catches the man in
the act of stealing its eggs and pushes him out of
the tree-top. As the man falls, he smashes the eggs
he collected for his wife. This tale is a multiform
of narratives 23, 37, 66B and 96, but while the pregnant woman comes to grief in the other tales, here it
is the husband who suffers.

90 Narrative No.103: this portrays how jealous
neighbours murder their more successful colleague.
It is a multiform of narratives 13, 60 and 92.

91 Narrative No.104: a story of how certain Baboons
kill a successful farmer in order to plunder his farm
afterwards. This is a multiform of narrative No.92,
the only difference being that in narrative No.104
the murderers are animals and not human beings. It
is also a multiform of narratives 13, 60 and 103.

92 Narrative No.105: a multiform of narratives 41,
71 and 99, only that here it is a bird, rather than
rats, which resuscitates itself after it has been
killed.

93 Narrative No.106: this portrays a selfish husband who will not share honey with his family during
a devastating famine. Instead he conceals the honey
and eats it secretly. It is a multiform of narratives 34 and 69. The man's family eventually discovers the secret store and they leave nothing for

the selfish head of the household.

94 Narrative No.107: an amalgamation of two stories
that do not always occur together in the tradition.
The first is an account of how all the beautiful
girls in a neighbourhood compete for the hand of a
handsome young man, but the girl who wins the contest
is the ugly one whose body is covered over by festering sores. This section of the narrative is a multiform of narratives 17, 22, 26, 48 and 53. The second
story is a tale about how a man acquires much wealth
because he possesses a magic wand, and is a multiform
of narrative No.44.

95 Narrative No.108: an account of a woman who
gives birth to a lump of stone. Whenever the woman
and her husband go to their farm, the stone turns
into a child and plays with other children in the
neighbourhood, but turns back into a lump of stone
before the parents return. Finally the parents realise what is happening and wait for the stone to
become a child, when they rush out from their hiding
place and capture the youngster. By so doing they
prevent him from ever turning back into a stone.

96 Narrative No.109: a combination of two stories
that do not always accompany one another in the tradition. The first is about young women who want certain ghosts, disguised as ordinary people, to marry
them. It is a multiform of narrative No.54. The
second story tells how a young boy constructs a magical drum and uses it to rescue his sister and her
companions from being killed by a monster. It is a
multiform of the second parts of narratives 25 and 40.

97 Narrative No.110: a story about a selfish young
man who swallows whatever food is set before him in
one gulp. When he eats the meal which his new bride
sets before him in this unseemly manner, the woman
becomes so frightened that she climbs a nearby tree
and refuses to come down. Her parents finally persuade her and take her home with them.

98   Narrative No.116:   an account of how a Wildcat
succeeds in winning brides for himself.   In this tale
a large monster-bird carries away a woman's three
beautiful daughters and deposits them in a tree-top.
When the mother of the stranded girls returns home
and finds out what has happened to her daughters, she
announces that whoever can bring the girls down
safely will be allowed to marry them.   The Wildcat
accomplishes the task and so marries the girls.

99   Narrative No.118:   a combination of two stories
that do not always occur together.   The first is about
a young man who marries a beautiful girl despite the
opposition of the mother-in-law.   The old woman is a
witch and has killed her daughter's five earlier
suitors.   This part of the tale is a multiform of
narrative No.20.
    The second part tells how the young man's dog kills
the witch who is about to destroy its master.   It is
a multiform of narrative No.37.

100   Narrative No.119:   a story of how a wicked old
man sets a trap to ensnare another man's son.   The
old man forces the young boy to stay on top of his
granary in order to keep out all possible marauders.
Although the tale ends inconclusively, it is reminiscent of narrative No.70, where a monster-bird steals
the food given to a boy who guards his father's farm.
The two tales may therefore be regarded as multiforms
of one another.

    On the basis of the major characters in these sum-
maries above, one may classify the tales into three
categories.   In the first group the principal characters are human or deceased human beings, while in the
second the main characters are animal.   The third
category is anomalous, because some of the major
characters in each tale are human and others animal.
    Tales whose major characters are human are by far
the most common in this cante-fable tradition.   In my
sample, this category constitutes approximately 70%
of the entire tradition, while tales with animals as
major characters comprise only about 18%.   Tales in

the anomalous category account for the remaining 12%.
As a result, one may conclude that the cante-fable
tradition is concerned primarily with the activities
of human beings.

The subject matter of the tales in which the principal characters are animal is limited in scope.
They are mainly concerned with the activities of Hare,
the trickster, and occasionally with those of
Tortoise, Lion, Frog and Chameleon. Animals that
resuscitate themselves after human beings have killed
them and monster-birds that eat women and children
also figure prominently in this group.

The subject matter of the tales in the mixed category are even more limited. Most of them deal with
the unnatural marriage of a human bride or bridegroom
to an animal spouse.

In the tales in which the principal characters are
human the subject matter is more varied, the most
memorable theme being that of the banishment of
children by their own parents. Other recurring topics in tales whose principal characters are human are:
a woman's maltreatment of the daughter of her dead
co-wife; the hatred of a more successful colleague;
the exploits of young girls who go to be tatooed or
to have their teeth removed according to ancient
Tonga fashion; the transformation of wood or blood
into marriageable women and their eventual transformation back again; various kinds of contests; people's
plight and reactions during a famine; and the journeys made by ordinary human beings to the land of the
dead.

CHAPTER II

LITERARY QUALITIES OF TONGA CANTE-FABLE

Contrary to current popular notions, the Tonga
cante-fable is a tradition of poetry, as will be
demonstrated in the following pages. On the basis of
the mode of performance, the genre may be divided
into two major parts: the declaimed section, and the
song portion. The second subdivision - the song - is
generally recognised as poetry, since the lyric of a
song is by definition poetry. This is exemplified by
the following song which is extracted from narrative
No.16:

> : Syawawa is not here
>   He has gone out
>
>   Syawawa is not here
>   He has gone out
>
>   There is a cock
>   Which crows at dawn
>   He has gone out
>
>   Ko - o!
>   Ko - O - Koliko
>   He has gone out
>
>   Ko - o!
>   Ko - O - Koliko
>   He has gone out :

What is often not realised is that the first section - the declaimed portion of Tonga cante-fable -
is also poetry. In the first place, the declaimed
sections have prosodic features that are normally
associated with verse. For example, an examination of
the first thirty-eight lines of narrative No.7 shows
that there are only five different line endings used
therein. A further study of the pattern of these
line endings reveals a remarkable rhyme scheme which
may be represented as follows:

```
a )
a )    Couplet

b )
b )    Couplet

a

c )
c )    Couplet

b )
b )    Couplet

d

c ─┐
c ─┤   Triad
c ─┘

a
d

a )
a )    Couplet

c
b
a
c
d

e )
e )    Couplet

a )
a )    Couplet

e
a
e    Duplicated Pattern
a

c
```

33

```
a - |
a - | Triad
a - |

b

c

a )
         Couplet
a )
```

Here there is end rhyme between the following pairs
of lines: 1 and 2, 3 and 4, 6 and 7, 8 and 9, 16 and
17, 23 and 24, 25 and 26, and between 37 and 38.
Furthermore, there is end rhyme among the following
triad of lines: 11, 12 and 13; and 32, 33 and 34.
Besides, the non-rhyming relationship between lines
27 and 28 is duplicated at the end of lines 29 and 30;
hence, they create the following Sequence:

```
a
e
a
e
```

The examination of the first thirty-eight lines of
the narrative No.7 shows that the lines rhyme mainly
in couplets, but sometimes in triads. What the analysis above demonstrates beyond any shadow of doubt is
that there is rhyme in the declaimed portion of this
typical Tonga cante-fable. Rhyme is one aspect of
poetry, but one must withhold judgement until one can
show that other aspects of poetry are found in this
section too.
   Further study of the genre shows that the basic
narrative unit of a Tonga cante-fable is the line
which invariably ends in the choral response:
Kalangati or *Kalungutu*, (we are listening) depending
on dialectal preference. This is exemplified in the
following passage taken from narrative No.50 of my
sample of the tradition:

34

Conteur	*Choral Response*
Kaniinga	Kalungutu
Kwali bantu	Kalungutu
Bali zyede mwana	Kalungutu
Oyo mwana wa'ali mubotu maningi	Kalungutu
Usi wakaya 'ukuweza	Kalungutu
Aunka kukuweza	Kalungutu
Kwaboola bayanda mwan' akwe	Kalungutu
(A long long time ago	Kalungutu
There were some people	Kalungutu
Who had a child	Kalungutu
That child was very beautiful indeed	Kalungutu
The father went out to hunt	Kalungutu
When he went out to hunt	Kalungutu
Some men came)	Kalungutu

As may be seen from the passage above, a line of Tonga cante-fable is not regular in terms either of the number of words or of the number of syllables found therein. For instance in the example above the first line comprises merely one word which is made up of only three syllables, while the fourth line comprises five words which are made up of thirteen syllables. Some lines in narrative No.7 comprise as many as seventeen words and forty-two syllables. Indeed a close examination of this tradition reveals that here a conteur is at liberty to compose his lines with as many words and therefore as many syllables as he pleases.

The genre is not stanzaic in form. On the contrary, it is stychic, based on line by line composition. Tonga cante-fable is also full of run-on lines, as may be seen in the following passage which is taken from narrative No.7:

Atwale maali	Kalangati
Bakaintu bobile aba	Kalangati
Bantumbukila antoomwe	Kalangati
(Having married two wives	Kalangati
The two women	Kalangati
Became pregnant at the same time	Kalangati)

35

Here the idea of the second line is carried over to the third.

Various aspects of parallelism are manifest in this tradition of cante-fable, as may be seen in the following examples:

Kwaali musankwa	Kalangati
Waatwele maali	Kalangati
Atwale maali	Kalangati
(There was a young man	Kalangati
Who married two wives	Kalangati
Having married two wives	Kalangati)

Here, the third line is almost an exact repetition of the second.

Umwi waazyala mwana omwe	Kalangati
Ono awo umwi waazyala babili	Kalangati
(One gave birth to one child	Kalangati
The other gave birth to two	
children	Kalangati)

Here there is a correspondence between the two lines above; both dwell on variations of child bearing.

The parallelism found in the genre is not restricted, however, to the repetition of words or ideas from one line to another. Sometimes there is internal repetition, where a word is repeated within one line, as is exemplified in:

Nkweenda mutumbu nkweenda	Kalangati
(The mother went and went	Kalangati)

Sometimes the repetition encloses a cluster of lines, marking them out as a large unit of narration. This is what is often called ring composition, since the repeated expressions form a ring round the cluster of lines. This is exemplified in the following passage:

Baba samika a mabbusu	Kalangati
A nsipa	Kalangati
Baba nanika kabotu-kabotu baba samika	Kalangati
(They dressed her up with shoes	Kalangati

36

With soap	Kalangati
They annointed her body very well	Kalangati
They dressed her up	Kalangati)

Here the lines are enclosed by *baba samika*.

Apart from parallelism, another feature of Tonga cante-fable is the presence of onomatopoeia, as in the following example:

Nditenge Kalangati
Kadidilika kana, kadidilika kana du Kalangati
(Choke me Kalangati
Kadidilika kana, kadidilika kana du Kalangati).

Kadidilika kana, kadidilika kana du depicts the manner in which Lweendo - one of the twins in the story - wrestles with his would-be foster-parent. They wrestle till the prospective foster-parent falls on the ground with a thud (*du*).

Another feature of the genre is the constant use of assonance and alliteration. This is due to some extent to the fact that as a Bantu language, Tonga has concordance between the verbs and the nouns as well as the adjectives in any given sentence or line, as is found in the following line:

Ono ebo ozyala bana bobile	Kalangati
(Now you have given birth to two children	Kalangati)

Here there is agreement between *bana* (plural) and *bobile* (plural).

Another example is as follows:

Ino walo woona buyo muli mukaintu omo ujisi mwana omwe	Kalangati
(Thereafter, he began to sleep in the house of the woman who had one child	Kalangati)

Here there is concordance between

walo (singular) and *woona* (singular).

Examples of assonance in the tradition are as follows:

Kwaali musankwa   Kalangati
Waatwele maali   Kalangati
(There was a young man   Kalangati
Who married two wives   Kalangati)

In the second line of the example above, the vowel sound of the initial syllable of the first word is the same as the vowel sound of the initial syllable of the second word of the line.

Another example of assonance in the genre is as follows:

Wakayumuka mukaintu oyo   Kalangati
(That woman set out   Kalangati)

Here, the fourth and fifth syllables of the first word have the same vowel sounds as the first and second syllables of the second word of the line.

Yet another example of assonance may be seen in the line below:

Kobweza bana aba ukabasowe   Kalangati
(Take these children and throw them
    away   Kalangati)

Here, the vowel sound of the last syllable of the first word is repeated six times in that single line of Tonga cante-fable.

Examples of the alliteration which also abounds in the tradition are as follows:

Kuti ime nsyikwe kucikonzya kayi koona
    bana boona akati   Kalangati
(I will not be able to sleep if the
    child sleeps in the middle   Kalangati)

Here the initial consonant of the first word is also the initial consonant of the fourth, fifth and sixth words of the line.

Another example of alliteration in the genre is found in the following line:

```
Baali basankwa balo                    Kalangati
(They were boys                        Kalangati)
```

Here the initial consonant of the first word occurs
as the initial consonant of the two other words that
make up the line.

What the examination above demonstrates is that
parallelism, ring composition, onomatopoeia, alliteration and assonance are aspects of the Tonga tradition of cante-fable. But these prosodic features are
aspects of poetry, rather than prose. Since all
these prosodic features are found in this tradition,
we may conclude that the Tonga cante-fable is a
poetic tradition.

What needs to be pointed out now is that the examples of prosodic features cited thus far in this
chapter were all taken from the first section of the
genre, that is, the declaimed portion in contrast to
the song section. Since rhyme, parallelism, ring
composition, onomatopoeia, alliteration and assonance are found in the declaimed section of this
genre, there is no doubt that this section also is
poetry.

A further proof of this is the ever-present choral
refrain - Kalungutu or Kalangati - found there. This
refrain is a distinct characteristic of the Tonga
tradition, and comes at the end of every line of the
declaimed section of the genre. Thus it both punc-
tuates and keeps the lines distinct from one another.
A refrain occurring with such regularity is characteristic of poetry.

Since the second portion of the cante-fable, the
song section, is already shown to be poetry, we may
conclude that the Tonga cante-fable as a whole
belongs to the poetic tradition.

The Form

Tonga cante-fables generally begin with an introductory piece, which sets the action of the narrative
in a time-frame when events that are generally considered impossible today were believed to have been
common-place happenings. These introductory pieces
are formalized openings and hardly ever change from

39

one narrative to another. They are expressed by the
formula: Kaninga or Mbukaninga (a long long time ago,
or once upon a time). Examples of such introductory
pieces or set openings are found in practically all
the narratives in my collection of the tradition.

Next comes a brief statement about the principal
characters of the narrative. This is exemplified in
Narrative No.85 (my collection).

There were a Hare and a Fox,	Kalungutu
Who were great friends.	Kalungutu
They even used to herd cattle together.	Kalungutu

Another example may be seen in narrative No.7 of my
collection:

There was a young man	Kalungati
Who had two wives	Kalungati

Yet another example may be seen in narrative No.13:

There were three men.	Kalangati
One used to feed his dog.	Kalangati
The other two had no dogs at all.	Kalangati

After the introduction of the characters, the next
section of the Tonga cante-fable is a brief statement
about the main action of the story. This is exemplified in narrative No.7:

Having married two wives,	Kalangati
The two women	Kalangati
Gave birth at the same time.	Kalangati
One gave birth to one child.	Kalangati
The other gave birth to twins.	Kalangati
When the husband came home,	Kalangati
How shall I sleep,	Kalangati
My wives?	Kalangati
Now you have twins	Kalangati
I do not love you any more.	Kalangati
I shall sleep in the house where there is only one child	Kalangati
Is this the way it should be done?	Kalangati
I shall not be able to sleep if the	

children sleep in the middle.	Kalangati
How can I sleep with you, sleeping like this?	Kalangati
So the young man,	Kalangati
Stopped going into the house where the twins lived.	Kalangati
He slept in the house where the wife had only one child.	Kalangati
Now the truth is that I do not love you.	Kalangati
You will bring dirt into my compound.	Kalangati
Take these children and throw them away.	Kalangati

It is such a statement that capsulates for the audience the subject matter of the narrative. Thereafter, the audience knows, as in the example above, that the story is about the banishment of twins.

Other illustrations of such brief statements in Tonga tradition of cante-fable may be seen from the following passage taken from narrative No.26 of my collection.

In that village	Kalangati
There was a young child	Kalangati
Who used to eat alone.	Kalangati
She used to live by herself.	Kalangati
She used to do everything all by herself.	Kalangati
She did not speak to anybody.	Kalangati
When the time for ploughing came,	Kalangati
She had her own field	Kalangati
Which she ploughed by herself.	Kalangati
So many animals	Kalangati
Wanted to marry her	Kalangati
But they were not able to do so	Kalangati
Because the girl could not talk.	Kalangati.

After listening to the passage above the audience knows immediately that the impending story is about the dumb girl and how she is married by the animal which forces her to utter her first spoken word. Hence, the audience realises that the impending narrative is a multiform of the theme of marriage.

41

The following example is taken from narrative No.40
of my collection:

They found the girls in a certain village	Kalangati
When the parents of the girls were absent from home.	Kalangati
It was the season for cultivating the land	Kalangati
And there were three girls left in the village.	Kalangati
When those young men arrived,	Kalangati
The girls rushed to them	Kalangati
And each chose the one she loved	Kalangati
And they took them home.	Kalangati
After they had taken the men into the house	Kalangati
The girls went and took a bath,	Kalangati
Then they brought something to drink	Kalangati
And offered it to the young men,	Kalangati
But those young men were Lions.	
They were not real people	Kalangati

Again once a traditional Tonga audience hears the
passage above, it knows immediately that what is to
follow is the story of the unnatural marriage between
Lions and some foolish girls. In other words, the
audience recognises that the impending story is a
multiform of the theme of marriage.

Yet another example of this kind of brief statement,
which summarises the main action of the story, is
taken from narrative No.50 of my collection:

One day her father went out to hunt.	Kalangati
Then people (who) wanted to marry her	Kalangati
Came	Kalangati
While her father was out hunting,	Kalangati
That girl lived in a house on top of some poles.	Kalangati
Whenever people came,	Kalangati
She refused to come down	Kalangati
Saying: you will abduct me and take me away from my father.	Kalangati

42

Here again, once the audience hears the statement above, it realises immediately that it is about to listen to a telling of the story of the abducted girl. In other words, the story to follow is a multiform of the theme of abduction.

One more example of the brief statement which generally precedes the main body of a Tonga cantefable comes from narrative No.54 of the same collection:

When they arrived there,	Kalangati
They stayed for a while.	Kalangati
At sunset they began their journey back to their residence,	Kalangati
While they were on their way,	Kalangati
They met a young man.	Kalangati
That young man was not a real human being.	Kalangati
He was a ghost.	Kalangati
The two girls began to follow the boy.	Kalangati

A traditional Tonga audience that hears the statement above knows immediately that what is to follow is the story of the unnatural love affair between a ghost and some foolish girls. This is evidently another multiform of the theme of marriage.

Of course a traditional audience has listened to numerous tellings of many multiforms of these topics. As a result, once a narrator announces his topic in the manner described above, his audience listens attentively to his narrative. This is the only way the audience can compare this telling of the narrative with the other tellings of the same subject matter within the audience's experience of the tradition. In this manner, the brief statement which precedes the main body of story is a narrative technique for heightening interest.

After this statement of subject matter comes the main body of the narrative, which is the full-length dramatization of the already-stated topic. The length of this section of the narrative depends entirely on the narrator's ingenuity, the nature of his audience, and the context in which the narrative takes place. If the narrator is highly experienced

in the tradition, has a keenly-interested audience
and a congenial atmosphere, for instance, he will
employ the numerous permissible organizational practices in order to create a long and interesting story.
Examples in my collection that readily come to mind
are narrative numbers: 16 and 20.

Narrative No.16 is a multiform of the theme of
abduction. Briefly, it is an account of how Seezimwe
- the monster - abducts and swallows Syawawa's wife,
while Syawawa is away on a distant journey. Before
setting out on the journey, however, the husband
instructs his wife to feed his guard-cock regularly.
The loud crowing of the cock protects the man's homestead by scaring away the menacing monster, Seezimwe.
So the safety of the wife depends on her meticulous
fulfilment of the condition stated above, and the
wife knows it. She indeed obeys the instruction at
first after her husband's departure. As the woman
continues to feed the cock, the bird's crowing
becomes louder and scares away the monster whenever
he approaches.

Not long afterwards, however, she begins to ignore
the husband's instruction by neglecting to feed the
cock. The more famished the cock becomes, the less
robust its crowing, and the monster notices this also.
Totally famished, eventually the bird dies; consequently, the monster abducts the negligent woman,
swallows her, and destroys her homestead. Distressed
on his return by the destruction of his home and the
absence of his wife, the husband searches tirelessly
for the monster. When Syawawa finally confronts the
monster and kills him by poisoning, he cuts open
Seezimwe's stomach and sets free not only his own
wife but all the other creatures that the monster has
swallowed. In a nutshell this is the story of narrative No.16.

But this is not the way the conteur presented the
material to his audience. Because this cante-fable
was performed during the cold, dry season after the
harvest - a time of general relaxation - the audience
was in a relaxed mood and had the time to listen to
long, entertaining narratives. Because the narrator,
Shabula Mwaanga, was experienced in the tradition he
had the potential to tell such a narrative. Hence he

employed various techniques to tell his complex story.

If we turn our attention to the summary of the story above we shall discover that it comprises the following principal parts:

(a) Husband's instruction
(b) Wife's disobedience
(c) Monster's visit to the village
(d) Monster's abduction of wife
(e) Husband's destruction of monster

An inexperienced narrator might have used these elements to construct a simple story. In this telling of the narrative (No.16), however, the third element - the monster's visit to the village - is skilfully repeated and amplified. During the monster's first visit to the village, the cock crows robustly and Seezimwe flees. During its second visit the cock's crowing scares away the monster once more. Thereafter the woman stops feeding the cock regularly. By the time the monster visits the village for the third time, the woman has reduced the food she gives to the cock. Consequently, the cock's crowing on this occasion is noticeably weaker. Even Seezimwe notices this too, especially as the cock crows twice as many times on this occasion as it did on the previous one. Reassured by the cock's diminishing strength, Seezimwe goes away again into his mountain dwelling. Meanwhile, the woman further reduces the amount of food she gives the cock. As a result, during Seezimwe's fourth visit the rooster has hardly any strength left. Nevertheless, it crows again. Thereafter the woman stops feeding the cock altogether; whereupon it soon dies. Consequently, when the monster returns the fifth time, the rooster cannot crow to scare him away. Frightened, the foolish woman sings again, hoping that the cock will crow, but the rooster does not respond. Petrified, she repeats the song three more times in the vain hope that the dead rooster will crow, but again the cock does not oblige. Enboldened by the silence of the rooster, the monster abducts the woman and swallows her. Thus the song is repeated five times during the monster's fifth visit. By so doing, the narrator skilfully prolongs the narrative.

But it is not only the visits themselves that are repeated, but also the songs occasioned by each visit. A closer study of the visits will reveal that the songs occur twice in the first vist; once in the second and third, although the cock's part on this occasion is repeated; once in the fourth, and five times in the fifth visit. The occurrence of these songs may be represented as follows:

Visits	Incidence of songs
1st	2
2nd	1
3rd	1 with a variation
4th	1
5th	5

It is noticeable that the song of the third visit entails a variation.

Even the second part of the story - the wife's disobedience - entails an element of amplification. The narrator does not merely tell his audience that the wife disobeys her husband's instruction. Instead he portrays the act of disobedience in four increasing stages of gravity. Finally the woman completely stops feeding the cock, in total disregard of her husband's instruction, and the bird dies.

The story of the abducted wife as narrated by this particular narrator on this occasion may therefore be represented as follows:

             a

             b   -   amplified 4 times

             c   -   repeated 5 times

             d

             e

where a = husband's instruction, b = wife's disobedience, c = monster's visit to the village, d =

monster's abduction of wife, and e = husband's destruction of the monster. It is the skilful use of the techniques of repetition and amplification which adds complexity to this narrative.

As has been mentioned earlier, excellence in cantefable composition in Tonga tradition is not limited to male story-tellers. Narrative No.20 is an excellent example of a Tonga woman's fine composition. It is also another example of a story composed by a talented narrator, who is highly experienced in the tradition, before a relaxed and keenly-interested audience.

Narrative No.20 is a multiform of the theme of marriage. Briefly, it is an account of how a wonderchild surmounts numerous magical tests and finally marries a wizard's daughter. Five suitors before him have died in the vain attempt to win the hand of the incredibly beautiful girl. But he sets out when he is only one day old, brings his wife home, and finally reveals his identity to his astonished parents. This simple tale is the crux of the narrative.

But as in narrative No.16, this is not the manner in which the story-teller presented the material to the audience on this occasion. Again this cantefable was performed during the cold, dry season after the harvest, and the audience was in a relaxed mood. The narrator on this occasion, Scholastica Mutinta, was also very experienced in the tradition, so that the situation was conducive to the composition of a long and entertaining narrative. What the narrator has done, therefore, is to take the simple story - whose outline is known to most members of the audience - and spin it into a complex narrative. She accomplished this by using the techniques of embellishment: duplication and amplification.

Narrative No.20 comprises the following main features:

(a) Vain attempts to marry beautiful girl
(b) Birth of bridegroom and his magical growth
(c) Bridegroom's ordeal
(d) Bridegroom's victory
(e) Bridegroom's return home with his wife.

47

An inexperienced story-teller might conceivably present it with little adornment to his audience. But Mutinta began her composition by recounting the details of the first two of the five disastrous earlier attempts made by the ill-fated suitors to win the hand of the witch's daughter. So here we have duplication. And the narrator could have recounted the details of each of these five earlier attempts, thereby making the story even longer. But she deliberately chooses to limit herself to two in order to shorten the story. As she says, 'The story is long anyway'. Thereafter, she elaborates the circumstances of the wonder-boy's birth by describing the traditional method of caring for new babies, the midwife's instruction to the mother of the wonder-boy, the way the new mother bathes the wonder-boy and the search for the wonder-boy. Then she equips the wonder-boy with the magical objects to help him surmount his ordeal before sending him on his journey.

Next, the story-teller skilfully repeats and elaborates the numerous ordeals which the wonder-boy surmounts. The first three take place at the home of the would-be parents-in-law. The first is that he should sit on a chair that magically kills people, while the second is that he should eat a poisoned meal. The last of the three is that he should bathe with poisoned water. But he triumphs in all three tests.

Next his future father-in-law takes him into a forest, asks him to climb up a palm tree, and magically makes the tree elongate itself. Here again the young boy uses his own talisman to overpower his prospective father-in-law. Frustrated, the old man brings the youngster home, where he again feeds him with poisoned food. But the wonder-boy uses his talisman to neutralise the poison once more. Unconvinced, the old man asks the young boy to drink poisoned sweet beer. But again, the wonder-boy triumphs.

Whereupon the prospective father-in-law lures the wonder-boy to the river and summons a crocodile to eat him. When even this fails to destroy the boy the old man finally recognizes the superiority of the youngster's talisman over his own. Now convinced of the wonder-boy's indestructibility, the old man takes

him home and shares a meal for the first time with
his prospective son-in-law. Finally the old wizard
reluctantly gives his consent to the proposed marriage between the wonder-boy and the wizard's beautiful daughter.

Accompanied by his new bride, the wonder-boy
returns to his own home; at first he is not recog-
nized, but he reveals his identity to his astonished
parents.

Thus we discover that it is the skilful use of
duplication, elaboration and variation that enables
this conteuse to transform the simple material at her
disposal into a complex narrative whose outline may
be represented as follows:

(a) Doomed Suitor - Duplicated 5 times - 1st Suitor
- 2nd Suitor
- 3rd Suitor
- 4th Suitor
- 5th Suitor

(b) Birth of Wonder-Boy

(c) Equiping of Wonder-Boy

(d) Wonder-Boy's bridal quest

(e) Ordeals - Duplicated with   - Chair
7 variations   - - Food
- Bath water
- Palm tree
- Food
- Sweet Beer
- Crocodile

(f) Wonder-Boy's victory

(g) Shared meal

(h) Father-in-law's consent

(i) Wonder-Boy's return home

(j) Wonder-Boy's epiphany

The song is a very important aspect of the main
body of the Tonga cante-fable, but this is not peculiar to Tonga tradition, since a cante-fable by

definition is a narrative whose component is a song. However, songs need not occur in every cante-fable in Tonga tradition; they are absent in narratives No.12 and 59 of my collection, for instance.

An example of the songs found in Tonga tradition of cante-fable is the following from narrative No.54:

Cantor: Girls go back
Chorus: I was decorated with a feather

Cantor: Girls go back
Chorus: I was decorated with a feather

C: This hat you see
C: Was put on me when I died
Ch: I was decorated with a feather

C: This tie you see
C: Was put on me when I died
Ch: I was decorated with a feather

C: This shirt you see
C: Was put on me when I died
Ch: I was decorated with a feather

C: These trousers you see
C: Were put on me when I died
Ch: I was decorated with a feather

C: These shoes you see
C: Were put on me when I died
Ch: I was decorated with a feather

Another is the song from narrative No.85:

Cantor: Where shall I take my mother
Chorus: Pengwa luwa luwa
C: Where shall I take my mother
Ch: Pengwa luwa luwa

C: I shall take her to many animals
Ch: Pengwa luwa luwa
C: There is a bird crying in the forest
Ch: Pengwa luwa luwa

C: Yes, my mother is gone
Ch: Pengwa luwa luwa

```
C:       Where shall I take my mother
Ch:      Pengwa luwa luwa
C:       Where shall I take my mother
Ch:      Pengwa luwa luwa

C:       I shall take her to many animals
Ch:      Pengwa luwa luwa
C:       There is a bird crying in the forest
Ch:      Pengwa luwa luwa

C:       Yes, my mother is gone
Ch:      Pengwa luwa luwa
```

Yet another example is the song from narrative No.7:

```
Cantor:  (Yaa!  It has fallen in the outside world
         (In the village of Nyanga Zumina
Chorus:  Yaa!  It has fallen
C:       Mawee!
Ch:      Yaa!  It has fallen at Loobwe

C:       (The father rejected the twins
         (Their graves he will throw away
Ch:      Yaa!  It has fallen
C:       Mawee!
Ch:      Yaa!  It has fallen at Loobwe

C:       (Yaa!  It has fallen in the outside world
         (In the village of Nyanga Zumina
Ch:      Yaa!  It has fallen
C:       Mawee!
Ch:      Yaa!  It has fallen at Loobwe
```

Most of the songs in the tradition are antiphonal
in nature, and are based on a call and response
interplay between a cantor and a chorus. Here the
narrator usually sings the part of the cantor, while
the participatory audience sings that of the chorus.

Repetition is a very common feature of the songs
in Tonga cante-fable. In the first stanza of the
song found in narrative No.54, for instance, both the
cantor's as well as the chorus' lines are repeated as
the second stanza of the song. It is also noticeable
that in the main body of this song it is only the
first line - which describes the item of clothing -

51

that changes, while the second and third lines of each stanza remain constant.

The songs occur several times within the main body of each narrative and are generally unaccompanied by any musical instruments. Like folksongs the world over, the melodies of the songs found in Tonga cantefable are usually simple. They are also fairly well known to most of the adults who participate in the narrative sessions.

After the main body of the narrative, the next section of a Tonga cante-fable is the conclusion. This is usually a statement informing the audience that the story has come to an end. Like the introductory piece, the conclusion is standardized and is generally expressed in such formulae as 'and that is the end of my story', 'I have come to the end of my story', or 'and this is all I have to say.' For instance, in narrative No.61 in my collection, we have:

This is the end of my story.

In narrative No.13:

And this is the end of the story.

In narrative No.20:

This is the story, my people. This is the end.

And in narrative No.50:

I have finished.

The last section of a Tonga cante-fable is the signature. This is an optional end of the narrative, and does not feature in all the stories in the tradition. In the numerous instances where the signature occurs, it is generally in praise of the narrator. For instance we have:

Narrative No.40:

I am Hancubezi who owns houses. I am the stories which eat meat, spread for the people and save the people.

Narrative No.61:

I am Juliana Muunda, the wife of Chief Choona.

Narrative No.49:

I am the child of Harry Nkumbula, child of Maambo.
I am the sister of Simon Kaila.
My kinsmen are as beautiful as the birds.
They work hard.
I am the daughter of Abraham Munsinde Maambo.
They bathe in milk.
They bathe in petrol.
Child of Ciinza.

The discussion above is a description of the gross
form of the Tonga cante-fable, portraying the linear
organization of the genre from the beginning to the
end of the narrative. In other words, it describes
the sequential order in which a narrator organizes
and links the various segments of his composition
from the introductory piece to the signature.
There is, however, another level of linking which
operates within the tradition. A narrator who has
to compose rapidly before an audience unites the
various segments of his narrative by a triadic or
sometimes duple arrangement of events or episodes.
This level of narrative organization is non-linear;
yet creates the tension of essences which make the
composition of a long narrative possible. Without
this level of organization, a narrator would have to
remember every little detail of a story before he
could compose it before his audience. As it is, when
he narrates one event which is part of a triad, he
will recall effortlessly the remaining events that
complete the triad.
The use of triads in narrative No.7 will be discussed fully in a later section of this investigation.
What needs to be demonstrated here is that this technique is not peculiar to narrative No.7. For this
purpose I shall use narrative No.40 which has a
different theme, and was recorded in Chief
Mwanachingwala's area of Mazabuka District, that is,
in another part of Tonga territory. Narrative No.40
is a multiform of the theme of marriage in this

tradition of cante-fable. Briefly it is the story of
three men who set out in search of prospective brides.
When they arrive at the home of three girls whose
parents are absent, the girls welcome the suitors and
soon set out with them for the men's home. A younger
brother of one of the girls insists on following them
despite his sister's beatings. So all seven arrive
at the suitors' home. At night as the girls sleep,
the young boy keeps watch over them, and is thus able
to see that their hosts turn into lions and devour
left-over bones. At dawn they become human again and
go out to hunt as before. This happens four times.
When the men are away, the young boy tells the girls
what he has seen at night, but his sister in particular refuses to believe him. Despite this, the young
boy realises how dangerous their predicament is, and
so begins to construct a wooden vessel (*Katendele*) as
a means of escape. Not long afterwards, the lions
decide to eat their brides, but the young boy manages
to take them one at a time into the *Katendele*, making
altogether four flights. The wooden vessel eventually carries the boy and the three girls to safety.
When they arrive home in their village, the parents
of the girls thank the young boy for having saved
their daughters. Finally, the boy narrates their
experience in the home of the Lions to the assembled
villagers.

Here there is an interplay between the triadic and
duple principle of composition. Firstly there is a
triad of girls who are left at home by their parents.
As the narrative progresses linearly, there is a
duplication of the triad, since the triad of girls is
married by a triad of boys. Thus the marriage of the
men to the girls produces a duple triad. The appar-
ent harmony that exists between the partners is
broken by the insistence of the young boy who accom-
panies the couples on their journey to the land of
the animals.

In the animal village, the men transform themselves
back into animals and hunt for their new brides
before they decide to eat the girls. This produces
two sets of duple hunting expeditions. In addition
the rescue vessel (*Katendele*) makes four - or two
sets of duple - flights before it rescues all the

54

endangered girls.

Towards the end of the narrative, the narrator
reverts to the principle of the triad again. The
village assembly at the end of the story comprises
three distinct groups: the boy, the girls whom he
rescued, and their parents who are grateful to the
young boy for his magical feat.

But this is not the only level at which the duple
and triadic principles operate. Indeed the narrative
itself can be divided into two major sub-divisions,
each of which may be further broken down into three
component parts. What is involved here, therefore,
is again an interplay between the duple and triadic
principles. The first sub-division is the men's
journey, while the second sub-division is the bride's
journey. The first sub-division is made up of the
following episodes: the quest for the brides; the
procurement of the brides; and the men's return to
their own homes. The pattern in this half of the
story is in keeping with the normal marriage pattern
in real Tonga life; we therefore expect everything to
go well for the newly-weds. But everything does not
go well for them in the end, for the husbands turn
out to be Lions. As a result, we have to look again
at the pattern of events in this part of the story
in order to find a traditional explanation for what
happens in the end. On closer scrutiny we find that
a marriage taboo has been broken; hence the misfortune. Good prospective brides in Tonga tradition
do not elope with strangers who propose to marry
them in the absence of their parents. As is the case
in many African societies, marriage in Tonga society
is a union of two extended families. It therefore
calls for the performance of elaborate rituals, the
first of which separate the new bride from her own
kinsmen. Then follow the rites of transition during
which the bride's mind is conditioned to accepting
not only her separation from those she has known
throughout her life, but also to accepting her
incorporation into the community of her new husband.
In this way the marriage of a Tonga bride gives the
community the opportunity to perform the rites of
passage which cushion the shocks that the bride is
exposed to as she migrates from one community to

another. These rites are not performed in narrative
No.40, and their neglect forebodes disaster for the
brides.

We should note that for the husbands the journey is
a fairly successful one, for they achieve their goal
of bride-procurement. There is a need for brides in
their village, and they succeed in bringing the human
brides from the human village to remedy the need of
their community. Three of them set out at the beginning of the story and they return home accompanied by
four other beings, making them seven, which is
believed to be the symbol of perfection. Thus in
this part of the story the human society functions as
wife-provider while the animal one functions as the
wife-receiver. The resolution of this part of the
story does show, however, that the Tonga consider
this an anomalous situation; hence the marriage is
aborted by the flight of the brides. The pattern of
this half of the story may be represented as follows:

Bridegroom's Journey

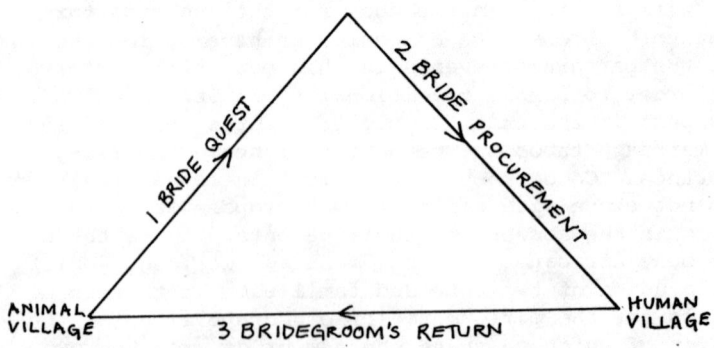

The bride's journey, which is the other half of the
story, begins with the bridal journey to the home of
the husbands. The next episode is the bridal sojourn
in the animal village and the final episode is the
bridal return home. This is a duplication of the
pattern of events in the men's journey; this bridal
journey which is the third episode in the first half

of the story now becomes the beginning of the bridal
journey, which is the second half of the cante-fable.
The bridal sojourn in the animal village is a substitute for the animals' stay in the human village,
while the bridal return to the human village is a
substitute for the men's initial journey to the human
village in search of some prospective brides. The
second half of the story - the brides' journey - may
be represented as follows:

Bride's Journey

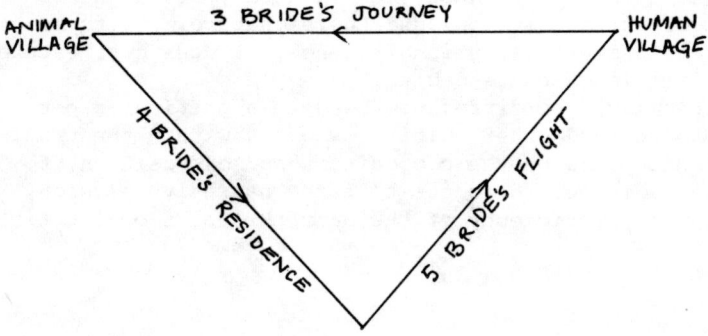

Here the human village is a substitute for the animal
village as the starting point of the journey, while
the animal village is a substitute for the human one
as the destination of the journey. The most significant difference between the duple set of journey
patterns is that while the return in the first half
of the story is the logical outcome of the quest for
a bride and is therefore intentional, the one in the
second half of the story is inconsistent with the
pattern of bridal journeys in real Tonga life.

The discussion above demonstrates that arranging
events in sets of triads and duples is used as a
compositional *aide de memoire* in narrative No.40.
The use of triads in narrative No.7, as a later section of this investigation shows, proves that the
device is not limited to narrative No.40 alone. On
the contrary, it is common practice in Tonga

tradition.

To recapitulate, the Tonga cante-fable is a tradition of poetry because it has such prosodic features as rhyme, alliteration, assonance, onomatopoeia, parallelism, ring composition and a recurrent refrain which are characteristics of poetry.

In terms of the mode of performance, the genre may be divided into two: the song portion, and the declaimed section. In terms of the form of the narrative as a whole, however, the genre comprises the following distinct parts: the introductory piece, the brief statement about the principal characters, the statement of theme, the main body of the narrative, the conclusion, and the signature. Of these, the signature is optional; hence, it does not feature in all Tonga cante-fables.

Finally, the difference between a particular performance and other multiforms of it within the tradition depends on the composition and disposition of the audience, the context of the narrative session, and the proficiency of the narrator as an oral artist.

CHAPTER III

DEFINITION OF THEMES

The story of the Banished Child, as noted in Chapter I, is one of the numerous tales encountered in the Tonga cante-fable tradition. Since every narrative in the tradition - as I shall demonstrate in the following pages - is defined by the habits of thematic composition witnessed in all other performances, a detailed examination of any one of these tales is a valid starting point in a study of the cante-fable tradition as a whole.

The story of the Banished Child was selected as the starting point in this investigation of the Tonga tradition for two major reasons. Firstly, it occurs frequently in the tradition. Secondly, it is a delightful story; hence, its popularity in the tradition.

Narrative No.7 in my collection, performed by Scholastica Mutinta, is the most fully developed as well as the longest multiform or telling of the story of the Banished Child which I was able to collect. It took the narrator approximately twenty minutes to perform and is by no means the longest cante-fable in the collection; No.20, performed by the same narrator, is longer by fully half. Nevertheless, as the most fully developed multiform of the story of the Banished Child in my sample of the tradition, it is a logical point of departure for an examination of this particular story in the tradition as a whole.

This does not mean that narrative No.7 is either the archetype or the 'correct' version of the tale of the Banished Child in Tonga tradition. On the contrary, I found no evidence either of an archetype or of any 'most correct' version of any narrative in Tonga oral tradition; hence, the term *multiform* will be used in preference to *variant* in this study, since variant implies the existence of a correct version from which the variants differ.

Throughout this investigation the term multiform is used mainly in its technical sense, to mean an individual performance or telling of a story which belongs to one tale-family with other tellings of the story in the given tradition. It is a particular enactment of a tale of a particular cante-fable plot. Multiforms resemble one another in certain important details.

An assemblage of certain motifs is characteristic of the tale of the Banished Child. I indicate the individual items in this motival complex by the device of underlining in the following synopsis of the tale as narrated by Scholastica Mutinta. These individual items are underlined only the first time that they are encountered in the synopsis.

Essentially, narrative No.7 - a transcription and translation of which appear as Appendices 1 and 2 - is the story of a young man who marries two wives. (Polygamy in traditional Tonga society as well as in many other traditional African societies is legal and commonplace.) The young man's two wives <u>give birth</u> to their children at the same time. The birth of their babies, however, occurs in the absence of their husband. One wife brings forth one son, while the other bears twin boys:

   Mbukaniinga#*
   Kwaali musankwa #
   Waatwele maali #
   Atwele maali #
   Bakaintu bobile aba #
   Baatumbiki (a) antoomwe #
   Umwi (w) aazyala mwana omwe #
   Ono awo umw (i) (w) aazyala babili #

   (Once upon a time #
   There was a young man #
   He married two wives #
   Having married two wives #
   The two women #
   Gave birth at the same time #
   One gave birth to one child #
   The other gave birth to twins #)

*The choral response, *Kalangati*, represented by this symbol, means 'We are listening'.

On the young man's return home, he repudiates the
wife who had twins:

Waboola mwanalumi #
Inino ndikoona buti Nubakaintu? #
Ono ebe ozyala bana bobile #
Nsyekuyanda pe #
Ndikoona muli moomu muli mwana omwe #

(The husband came home #
How shall I sleep, my wives? #
You have two children #
I do not love you anymore #
I shall sleep in the house where there is only
  one child #)

The repudiated wife protests against her husband's
decision, but to no avail. The husband finally
banishes the twins, commanding that they be left to
die in the forest:

Kobweza bana aba ukabasowe #
Kufumbwa nkoyanda ambweni ukabatule kwenu#

(Throw those children away into the forest #
If you like take them to the home of your
  parents #)

Compelled to exile her children from her home, the
mother of the twin boys journeys to the forest where
she conceals her sons in a rock-cave on a river-bank;
thus, offering them non-dietary provision or donation.
On her return, she becomes the favourite wife of the
husband, but unknown to the man, she travels to the
forest regularly in order to provide her banished
sons with nourishment, which is another form of donation. Meanwhile, she deceives her husband into
believing that she has killed her twin sons. Thus,
the twins manage to survive.
    One day, when the twin sons have reached adoles-
cence their mother neglects to feed them at the right
time:

61

```
Ino obo buzuba #/
Bakacelwa cifumo-fumo
   Ati ma!  (mbo)ndakasiya zyakulya mbobalya
     Sunu ndaunka kumazuba #
```

```
(one day #
She was late in the morning
  Oh dear!  I left them food there
    Today I shall go in the evening #)
```

Meanwhile, a benevolent spirit who has only one eye,
one hand, and one leg adopts the twins who live in
the wild. Before the spirit adopts the twins, however, he challenges them to a contest of wrestling.
By throwing him, each twin qualifies for adoption by
the spirit, who takes them to live in a comfortable
mansion in the forest.

While the twin boys live in their new home, their
mother journeys to their old cave dwelling to bring
them food, but on failing to find them she fears that
they are lost. She searches everywhere for them and
when on a subsequent journey to the cave she does not
find them, she laments their loss:

```
(I)nsondo yaakumana #/
(I)no bamane banyina baboola nibaleta zyakulya #/
Batiti kulanga-langa #
Wabayaya bakomena kale bana bangu
  Syena mulum(i) (w) angu waka ndeena? #/
Waunka mutumbu kumesyo nkuya bulila #/
Waunka uya bulila.  Akasike kumaanda oko #/
```

```
(A week later #
The mother set out and took them food #/
She looked everywhere #/
But did not find them #/
She looked everywhere #/
Someone has killed my grown up children.
  Did my husband deceive me #/
The mother began to cry #/
She began to cry.  Later she returned home #/)
```

Having thus mourned the twins whom she imagines to
be dead, the woman sets out for the forest, this time

to seek some evidence of what has happened to them.
All of a sudden she finds an·impressive mansion in
the forest. Fearing that its occupants may harm her,
she begs them to spare her life. The occupants of
the house are no other than her own twin sons whom
she had presumed were dead, but she does not recog-
nise them. Even when they reveal their identity to
her, she doubts that they are indeed her children.
Finally, she recognises the two young men who stand
before her as her two lost sons:

Balisukata.
    Syena uli mukuwa okakala abana? #/
Wazwa kale Lweendo #/
Ikuti ndiswe baama #/
Ndiswe baniini biya. Kamuboola kamuzya buyo
    mwiimikile awa
        Ndendiswe sikuulu kumwi nguwaa tutolede #/
Wakaa kutupa zyoonse zyibelesyo mbuli
        Mukuwa muta yoowi. Kwaamba ndiza mundijaye
    teesyi? Nkuti ndendiswe #/
Bakaima geeti. Mbabana bangu #/
Bamunjizya mucembele mung'anda,
Yalila nguluulu.mizinga. Nkuti mutalijayi #/
Impenzi lyamana #

(She braced herself.
    Are you the rich man living with my children? #/
Lweendo had already come out #/
It is us, mother #/
We are the little ones. Come and stand here.
    It is us. The one-legged spirit took us #/
He gave us all the tools, just like a rich man.
    Why are you afraid?
Perhaps you will kill me, thinking that I am not
    the one. It is us #
They stood at the gate. These are my children! #/
They made joyful sounds. You must not kill
    yourself #
My troubles are over #)

As a way of welcoming their mother to their forest
home, the twins ask her to take a bath. After this
act of purification they dress her in new clothes and

63

thus transform her into the beautiful woman she used
to be. Then they proceed to burn her old clothes.
This act reinforces her earlier purification and
transformation.

After the woman's delightful stay, her twin sons
give her a dish which contains some delicious food,
and as they escort her back to the edge of the forest
they instruct her to behave well towards their father
despite his previous illtreatment of her. Elated by
all the good things that have happened to her, she
bursts into a song. She sings about the paradoxical
fate of her twin sons; the forest which was to have
been their grave has now surprisingly turned out to
be the source of their wealth and good fortune:

    Yaa kuwa ko Syimutema-Mbalo
    Ku munzi Nyanga zumina
    Yaa kuwaa
    Kawee!
    Yaa kuwa koo loobwe.

    Taata mbakakaka maanga
    Zyuumbwe zyini a kasowe
    Yaa kuwaa
    Mawee!
    Yaa kuwa koo loobwe.

    Yaa kuwa ko Syimutema-Mbalo
    Ku munzi Nyanga zumina
    Yaa kuwaa
    Mawee!
    Yaa kuwa koo loobwe.

    (Yaa! It has fallen in the outside world
    In the village of Nyanga Zumina
    Yaa! It has fallen
    Mawee!
    Yaa! It has fallen at Loobwe.

    The father rejected the twins
    Their graves he will throw away
    Yaa! It has fallen
    Mawee!
    Yaa! It has fallen at Loobwe.

    Yaa! It has fallen in the outside world
    In the village of Nyanga Zumina
    Yaa! It has fallen
    Mawee!
    Yaa! It has fallen at Loobwe.)

On her return home, she deceives her husband as to
the source of the food which she has brought with her.
She tells him that her father killed a cow, sold some
part of it in the nearby urban centre and was thus
able to provide her with all the goods she brings
home. The husband is delighted with what his wife
has brought home, and after receiving some instruction from her as to how to hold his cup of tea, he
washes his hands (another act of purification) and
sits down to the meal his wife provides.

Soon afterwards, the woman journeys to the forest
again to visit her sons, who this time accord her a
military reception, causing her to burst again into
her song. As in her last visit, she takes a purificatory bath. This time, however, her old clothes -
presumably the ones her children gave her during her
first visit - are washed and not burnt like the old
ones she wore during her first visit. This shows the
superiority of the things which emanate from the
forest over the ones that originate in the village;
the clothes from the forest may be purified by being
washed, while the ones from the village can be purified only by being burnt.

As in her first visit, the mother is again given a
set of new clothes and she receives further instruction - only this time the instruction is about how to
apply facial cosmetics, while the first concerned her
relationship with her husband. During her first stay,
she tells her sons of their father's intention to
expel his other wife, and tells them too about his
suspicion that she has another lover who he fears
offers her the goods she brings home. This makes one
realise that her husband did not in the first
instance really believe her story as to the source of
the goods she brings home.

In the evening, she sets out for her home in the
village and as before happily sings about the paradox
of her children's good fortune. On her arrival home,

she unpacks her baggage and provides her husband with the food she has carried home from the forest. In addition, she also gives him the new clothes her sons have given him. Thus she is an intermediary between her sons, who are donors, and her husband who is the recipient of the goods. In another respect, she duplicates the role of her sons; they instruct her on several aspects of life and she, in turn, instructs her husband, firstly on how to hold his cup of tea and secondly on his relationship with his other wife. Again, the transformation the husband undergoes at home is akin to that which the wife experiences in the forest.

The husband, who imagines that he now knows the home of the lover who provides his wife with the goods, now gives vent to his jealousy. He tells his wife that he is afraid that her new lover will one day take her away from him, but the wife reassures her husband that nobody can take her away. Thus reassured, the husband expels his other wife and her son despite the advice of the mother of the twins. This provokes the mother of the twins into instructing her husband once more.

Not long afterwards, the mother of the twins journeys into the forest again to visit her children for the third time. On this occasion, however, her husband asks his friends to come along with him to attack his wife's seducer. He instructs them, however, not to harm his wife; he plans to live with her in the lover's home after he has killed the owner of the mansion.

As the father and his men wait in ambush, his wife goes by singing her song, unaware of the presence of her husband and his men. Soon after her entry into the forest mansion, her husband and his accomplices attack the home of the presumed lover of his wife, but the defenders defeat them easily and then invite them into their home where they prepare a feast for their father and his men. Eventually, the twins reveal their identity to the invaders; whereupon, their father's companions mock him for mistaking his own sons for his wife's lovers. Thoroughly ashamed of his action, the man begs his children to forgive him and in this way becomes reconciled to his

banished sons. Finally, the man, his sons, his wife
and all companions return to their home in the village where the man prepares a feast to welcome home
his banished sons. In this manner, he <u>reintegrates</u>
them into the village life. This feast is evidently
a duplication of the one the twins prepare for their
father and his men in the forest.

The above is a presentation of the sequential order
of the events in the narrative and portrays one level
of organization of the narrative structure. Levi-
Strauss suggests that there is yet another possible
level of structural organization of myths.[3] This
appears to be true of Tonga cante-fables, as will be
demonstrated later.

The ability of the story-teller to maintain the
balance among the various characters in the narrative
while at the same time sustaining the linear progression of the main action of the tale is a
remarkable aspect of this cante-fable and I shall now
explore the elements that help in this.

Triads seem to be an important element in helping
to maintain the balance among the characters as well
as the episodes in the narrative, for things occur in
groups of threes in this tale. First, there is the
marital triad of a man who is married to two wives.
This triad produces a triad of offspring - a single
child and twin boys. As the narrative progresses
linearly, there is yet another triad, comprising the
mother and her twin sons in the forest. The adoption
of the twins generates another triadic arrangement,
consisting of the twins and their foster-father.

The scene in which the mother finds her lost children generates another triad - the mother and her twin
sons. On closer examination, one begins to realise
that the details of the second mother-offspring triad,
which I shall call the triad of the mansion, are
similar in many respects to the events in the first
mother-offspring triad, which I shall label the triad
of the cave. The qualitative difference between the
two reflects not only the linear progression of the
narrative but also the change in the fortunes of the
banished twins. In the triad of the cave, the banished twins are totally helpless and are provided for
by their mother. In the triad of the mansion,

however, the previously helpless twins are now not only grown up men but also very wealthy. Moreover, the twins who were the recipients in the triad of the cave are the donors in the triad of the mansion, while their mother who functions as the donor in the earlier triad is the recipient in the latter triad.

The journey the mother makes in order to visit her twin sons in the forest generates yet another triad, which will be labelled the visitation triad. The objective of the first journey in this triad is to seek the evidence that will convince her that her sons are indeed dead. Instead of finding any evidence of death, the mother finds her twin sons alive and well. Her second visit to her sons' forest dwelling is uneventful in that its outcome is predictable from the very beginning. Here the sons entertain their mother and as before offer her many material goods to take to her home in the village. But the outcome of her third visit is in many ways as unpredictable as that of her first. Instead of the peace and quiet which she has come to expect from her visits to her sons, she and her hosts are attacked by her husband. Furthermore, when the husband sets out to ambush the presumed lover of his wife, his intention is to kill the man who has seduced her. In the end, the husband and his colleagues are not only defeated, but the occupants of the mansion turn out to be his own children rather than the alien seducers of his wife which he mistakenly believed them to be.

These are the instances of the use of the triad in the tale under review. The triad is a useful narrative tool in these instances because it helps the narrator to organize her story. When she begins to narrate one episode which she remembers as part of a triad she is able effortlessly to recall the other episodes that comprise the triad.

Composing in triads, however, is not the only narrative technique employed by this narrator. Interplay between the village and the forest as the setting for the events is yet another technique discernible in narrative No.7. In this way the tale highlights the contrast between the village and the forest that is also noticeable in real Tonga life.

The home village is the setting for the events that
take place at the very beginning of the narrative.
Here the home symbolizes marital discord, since the
young father is so obsessed with his concern for
cleanliness that he banishes his twin sons for fear
they may dirty his home. From here, the setting
shifts to the forest. The twin babies are taken to
the forest cave on the bank of a river. In this context, the forest becomes the symbol of refuge. Later
when the half-being adopts the twin sons and installs
them in his forest mansion, the forest begins to
represent not merely a place of refuge but a luxur-
ious dwelling as well. The forest is the setting for
the visitation triad. During this phase of the
narrative the twin boys who inhabit the forest mansion cater for their parents who live in the village.
Thus the forest symbolizes the source of instruction
and material goods, while the village symbolizes the
lack of these good things. The scene then shifts
back to the home which is being enriched by goods and
instruction from the forest. In this case, the
forest symbolizes the source of acculturation, and
the village the process of acculturation.

The next scene is the forest, where the mother is
given a very formal initial reception and another set
of instructions - she must not allow anyone to accompany her when she visits them; the forest still represents a place of instruction. The scene then
shifts to the home. Here the behaviour of the wife,
who is now totally indoctrinated into the sophistica-
ted manner and right conduct of the forest, contrasts
sharply with the mean behaviour of her husband. The
home thus represents socially unacceptable conduct.
The scene next shifts again to the forest, which is
once more the place of filial hospitality and the
setting for the reconciliation between the father and
the twin sons whom he has banished. Hence the forest
in this context symbolizes the restoration of the
familial harmony that was lacking at the beginning of
the narrative. The concluding scene takes place at
home, which has now become the symbol of not merely
familial bliss but also of communal harmony. This
completes the circle of events that begins at home,
then shifts to the forest and finally returns to the

home.

Viewed in this manner, the contrast between the home and the forest is an effective narrative tool. One pair of contrasts begets another, because the second part of one is the first component of a new contrasting pair, which in turn begets yet another. As a result, a talented storyteller, who has thoroughly mastered the contrasting situations permissible in the tradition, needs only to think of one episode, and a series of events falls into place almost effortlessly.

The final scene seems to imply that, although the forest has represented the source of instruction, material goods, and familial harmony throughout the narrative, it is nevertheless an anomalous human habitation. By implication, it suggests that the sophistication and right conduct which belong here should rightly belong to the home instead. Seen in this light, the narrative begins to resemble a rite of passage, as described by van Gennep[4], in that its main action entails a separation, a transition, and a reincorporation. The banishment of the twins to the forest involved their sequestration from the rest of the society. The time the twins spend in the forest is analogous to a transitional period. During this phase of their lives, the twins are betwixt and between the world of ordinary people and the magical world of their half-being foster-parent. The feast which the father prepares for his returning twin sons resembles a rite of incorporation in that the banished sons who have grown up entirely in the forest are now formally accepted as *bona fide* members of the community. It is thus very tempting to conclude from the above exposition that this cante-fable is the narrative accompaniment to a rite of passage. Perhaps it performed such a role at some time in its distant past. There is nothing, however, in the performance of narrative No.7 or in the Tonga cante-fable tradition to suggest that this tale is now part of a ritual.

In addition to the triad and the contrast between home and forest, the song is another narrative tool employed in this tale. Torrend suggests that because the songs play a prominent role in Tonga cante-fables

70

the people indeed use the cante-fables merely as a pretext for entertaining themselves with songs.[5] This assumption, which is echoed by Ruth Finnegan[6], implies that the songs are not integrated into the narrative structure of the cante-fables and that the songs appear whenever the raconteur pleases. This may be so in some African cante-fables and in some Tonga ones for that matter, but is not true of all Tonga cante-fables, as an examination of the role of the song in narrative No.7 will show. This will enable us to deduce a more plausible role of the song in the tradition as a whole. We have not only to examine the meaning of the song itself but also to scrutinize the narrative session as a whole. This tale, like others in Tonga tradition, is narrated at night after a good meal following a good day's work during the cold dry season, when people have all but harvested their maize crops. As they sit by the fireside in the cold winter night listening to tales, the audience is apt to fall asleep. Naturally, when this happens the narrator loses their attention. The participation of the audience in the narrative session by responding 'kalungutu' after each major cadence, in addition to joining in the singing of songs, helps keep people awake.

Besides helping to keep the audience awake, the songs also entertain them. But these two functions are incidental to the structure of the narrative. Hence, if they were the only roles performed by the song in this tale, the song would indeed be incidental to narrative No.7. A closer examination of the song, however, shows that it has a profound meaning, which suggests that it plays another role besides that of entertainment. The song rejoices over the paradoxical fate of the twin sons who acquire great wealth in the forest which was initially supposed to have been their grave. Thus the song sums up the events in the narrative and even points to a possible source of resolution of the major crisis in it.

The song occurs four times in the tale and the positioning of each song is not accidental. On the contrary, each song marks a unit of meaning. Indeed, the song divides the narrative into five meaningful units, as may be seen in the following illustration:

71

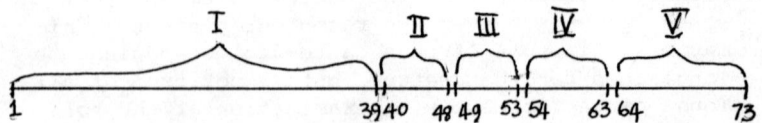

There are seventy-three incidents in the entire
narrative, and the song appears after the thirty-ninth
incident, after the forth-eighth incident, after the
fifty-third incident, and after the sixty-third incident.

The period from the first incident to the thirty-
ninth - phase I - represents that of greatest marital
discord in the narrative. This is the time when the
young father orders his twin sons to be thrown away.
Phase II, bounded by incidents forty and forty-eight,
is the period when the good things from the forest
are beginning to affect the disorganized situation at
home. Phase III, bounded by incidents forty-nine and
fifty-three, is the period when the influence of the
forest on the village deepens. During this period
the wife does not only bring home items of food; she
also brings home tea, which in the context of the
fable is considered an item of greater sophistication
than ordinary food. Phase IV, bounded by incidents
fifty-four and sixty-three, marks the contrast between the wife's socially acceptable behaviour and her
husband's base conduct. It is the final storm before
the calm. Phase V, bounded by incidents sixty-four
and seventy-three, is the period of reconciliation
between father and banished sons. In this phase, the
father renounces his socially unacceptable behaviour
and then reintegrates his sons into the society from
which they have been banished.

Thus the songs repeated on four separate occasions
mark the boundaries of meaning of the various phases
of the tale. But the songs do not merely punctuate
the narrative; they are themselves vehicles of meaning. By restating the central idea of the narrative

at the critical moments of transition between phases,
the song updates the audience on the sense of the
narrative. In addition, by pointing to a possible
source of the resolution of the central crisis of
the tale, it prepares the audience for what lies
ahead. As a result, it crystallises the past and yet
spurs the audience to listen even more attentively in
order to learn how the issues already summarized in
the song are to be resolved. Thus the song is a
paridigm of the entire cante-fable. Since it plays
these various roles, and above all is an instrument
of meaning, it may therefore be concluded that it is
an integral part of the narrative structure of narrative No.7 and not merely a voluntary embellishment.

The tale of the Banished Child as portrayed in narrative No.7 is not an isolated one. There are six
other tales in my collection which resemble one
another to such a degree that I have grouped them
together as belonging to one tale-family or as shar-
ing a common cante-fable plot. These are Nos.6, 18,
21, 46, 56 and 100. A comparison of even the introductory portions of these cante-fables is sufficient
to show that the tales are multiforms of one another.

In the introductory section of narrative No.7, a
young man marries two wives. His wives conceive at
the same time and give birth simultaneously. One
gives birth to twin boys, while the other gives birth
to one boy. This introduction bears striking resemblance to the introductory portion of narrative No.6,
in which a young man also marries two wives. One of
his wives gives birth to twins and one of them dies,
while the other wife bears five children and they all
live. The central idea in the two introductory portions is that of a young man, his marriage to two
spouses, and the birth of children to each of the
wives. No.7 is more detailed, since it mentions the
pregnancy of the wives and describes the circumstances of the childbirth of each wife - details
which are absent in No.6. Despite these differences,
the details of the two introductory portions show
that they are the beginnings of the same story.

The introductory section of No.46 is also similar,
for it too begins with a young man who marries two
wives. Both wives become pregnant simultaneously,

73

but he prohibits the birth of a baby girl. These two
wives also give birth to their babies at the same
time - one bearing the prohibited girl. As a result,
one may conclude that this narrative resembles Nos.6
and 7, although it is more akin to 7 than to 6 in
that 7 and 46 mention the pregnancy of the wives and
their simultaneous childbirths. Even so, the introductory sections of narrative Nos.46 and 7 are not
identical because in No.7 one wife gives birth to one
boy and the other gives birth to twin boys, while in
No.46 one wife bears a boy while the other bears a
girl.

The introductory section of No.21 also resembles
those of the three preceding tales, for here again a
young man marries two wives. Soon after he prohibits
the birth of girls in his household, his two wives
become pregnant at the same time. In his absence,
one wife gives birth to a boy while the other gives
birth to a girl.

Although the introductory section of No.56 is
rather brief, it too bears remarkable resemblance to
that of the four preceding multiforms: a man marries
two wives and one of them gives birth to a boy while
the other gives birth to a girl.

The details of the introductory portion of No.100
are similar in many respects to those of the five
preceding multiforms, for in this, too, a man marries
two wives who later become pregnant. Soon after he
prohibits the birth of a girl, one of his pregnant
wives gives birth to a boy while the other bears him
a girl.

Although the introductory section of No.18 is very
brief and its details different in several respects
from those of the six preceding narratives, still it
bears resemblance to them. In it, a man impregnates
a woman (presumably his wife), who conceives and
bears twins.

From the analysis of these seven multiforms, one
may deduce that the central idea of the introductory
sections of the tale of the Banished Child has the
following elements: a young man, his polygamous marriage to two women, their simultaneous impregnation
and conception, the husband's prohibition of the
birth of twins or girls, his absence, and the

simultaneous childbirth of the two women. One woman
gives birth to a desired boy while the other bears a
prohibited girl, or bears one child while her co-wife
gives birth to twins.

As is usual in the analysis of multiforms, none of
the introductory sections of any one of the seven
multiforms in my sample has all the elements of the
central idea. Indeed the elements which constitute
the central idea may be likened to the building-
blocks which a mason uses in order to construct an
edifice. Like a mason, a story-teller utilizes only
the building-blocks that he needs in order to construct his multiform. Each of the seven narrators
constructs his or her tale by using some building-
blocks identical to the ones used by the other six,
showing that the seven introductory pieces are the
various beginnings of the same tale. This also vali-
dates my earlier provisional classification of all
seven as multiforms of one another.

But before one can be confident that the seven
narratives are actually multiforms of one another, it
is necessary to analyse the remaining portions of the
seven tales in order to devise a reliable classificatory system. This, however, presents formidable tax-
onomical problems. Unfortunately, there is no reliable taxonomy of Tonga cante-fables to guide us here.
Torrend's anthology,[7] which contains the most worth-
while research in the tradition, is not precise
enough for this project. Torrend generally uses
catchwords - usually 'the first verse of the principal song'[8] - as the titles of the tales in his
anthology of Tonga folklore. As his justification
for doing so, he claims that the Tonga themselves
differentiate the tales by such a device.

The intervening half-century between Torrend's
research and the present work make it impossible to
verify the assertion with any of the narrators whose
narratives are included in Torrend's anthology. Many
of those encountered by the present investigator,
however, remember their narratives not only by catch-
words or catch-phrases but by other devices as well -
the chief of which is the recapitulation of the
central idea of the narrative itself. Furthermore,
not all the tales in Tonga tradition contain a song,

so that the use of the first verse of the song as the tale's title is an unsatisfactory classificatory device.

Because many of the story-tellers whom I encountered remembered their narratives when they were furnished with the central ideas of the tales, it is tempting to base the system of classification on this, thus giving the impression that the resulting terminology derives from the indigenous narrators themselves. But any taxonomy based on such a device will ultimately be as unsatisfactory as Torrend's, as there is hardly any known indigenous consensus for the central idea of any Tonga oral narrative. The objective of the present study is to evolve a classificatory system which is a precise and effective analytical tool, and such a system can be devised by breaking down the seven multiforms of the story of the Banished Child into their component elements, as has already been done with their introductory sections.

The resulting constituent units or building-blocks - examples of which may be seen in the earlier analysis of the introductory sections - are analogous to the themes of oral epic. In this work, the term *theme* is used in the sense in which it was conceived by Milman Parry, defined by Albert Lord and refined by David Bynum to be 'a conglomeration of narrative matter in oral epic tradition which recurs in the tradition, and which is discrete because some of its occurrences have no consistent sequential relationship with other such units.'[9] Perhaps the only modification that needs to be made to the above definition is to point out that themes do not operate exclusively in the oral epic; they operate in the oral cante-fable also.

The building-block, Birth, which is a component of the central idea of the tale of the Banished Child, will serve as the starting point of this exploration of the themes of Tonga cante-fables, because it occurs in various forms in all seven multiforms. In exploring the nature of this and other building-blocks in the tradition I shall not limit myself to the seven multiforms of the story of the Banished Child. On the contrary, I shall explore the nature of such building-blocks throughout the tradition, as

represented by the hundred cante-fables which constitute my sample.

It is important to explore the nature of these
building-blocks in the tradition as a whole because
this is in keeping with the listening habits of a
traditional audience, which has generally heard
several possible multiforms of any given traditional
building-block, and therefore habitually recognizes
the given building-block in its numerous forms. Thus
when a traditional audience listens to a particular
story-teller, it visualizes not merely the specific
form of a building-block which the narrator chooses
in his telling of the tale; each member of the audience visualizes as many of the protean forms of the
building-block as are known to him. This explains
why the members of an audience do not derive uniform
enjoyment from the same narrative; the level of
entertainment each derives is directly proportional
to his level of knowledge of the entire tradition as
well as his ability to recall past experiences of it.
As a result, a cante-fable narrated to a traditional
audience is analogous to a parable; each listener
derives as much from it as he brings to it.

Turning to the building-block, Birth, one notices
that besides its appearance in the seven multiforms
of the tale of the Banished Child - narratives No.6,
7, 18, 21, 46, 56, 100 - it also occurs in twenty
other narratives in the sample: Nos. 1, 2, 5, 11, 20,
23, 34, 43, 47, 53, 74, 75, 80, 90, 97, 106, 108, 110,
and 118. All twenty-seven instances of this building-
block in the sample will be the basis of my exploration of the nature of this particular building-block
in Tonga tradition.

Based on a lengthy examination of the twenty-seven
instances of Birth in the sample, I have come to the
conclusion that there are two major kinds of Birth
occurring in Tonga cante-fable tradition. The first
is the sexual type, in which a married person or
animal conceives and later gives birth to a child.
The second is the asexual type in which a woman and
her reproductive organs need not be involved. I
shall discuss the second type first.

The asexual births in Tonga cante-fable tradition
consist of two major subtypes. In the first subtype,

77

as may be seen in narrative No.11, a woman collects her non-menstrual blood - often blood from her leachings - and covers it in a pot. After a while - one month in narrative No.11 - the blood transforms itself into a child. This subtype of birth may be regarded as a symbolic representation of the natural birth process. The pot represents the woman's womb; while the blood represents the zygote which turns into a human baby after the gestational period.

Since this subtype of birth appears to be a symbolic duplication of normal human birth, one expects the children born through it to be as varied as in real human births. Thus one expects that some would be male and some female; some twins and some born one at a time. Such, however, is not the case in Tonga cante-fable tradition. The tradition seems to limit not only the possible number of babies born though this process, but also the sex of the offspring as well. Twins do not seem to be born in this manner, nor do boys; only girls can be born, one at a time.

The second type of asexual birth in the tradition is more fantastic. An example of this is narrative No.19. Here an old woman consults a diviner in order to find out the reason why her son whistles all the time. The diviner instructs her to carve a tree, and she carves the image of a girl which three weeks later turns into a living girl. In No.19 as well as another multiform, No.57, a feather functions as the girl's life-centre. The act of installing this feather or a tuft of hair on the figurine transforms it from lifeless wood into a human being. In some instances the carver animates the figurine by breathing onto it. This is akin to the giving of life by breath in the biblical creation myth in Genesis, and is a classic example of homeopathic magic.

In theory, the result of this process of creation in Tonga tradition could be as diverse as in real life; hence, one expects that men and women, boys and girls, single and multiple births would result from it. But once again this is not what happens in the cante-fable tradition. The tradition seems to restrict the possible options quite rigidly. Only marriageable girls - *kore* - are created through this process in this tradition.

78

Thus in Tonga cante-fable tradition, the possible
offspring resulting from an asexual birth is usually
a girl, who frequently becomes the wife of the principal character of the narrative. In all the multiforms in the sample, she is later abducted from her
husband's home when the husband is away hunting or
looking for honey, and the husband searches for her
on his return. In narrative No.19 the husband is
afraid that his neighbours may kidnap his wife and so
gives her a gourd full of millet. When the abductors
kidnap her, she drops the millet along the path. Her
husband follows the path marked by the millet and
finally reaches the home of the wife's kidnappers,
where he pulls out the feather which is her life-
centre and in this way transforms her into her
original wood. This is the fate of all the offspring
resulting from this type of birth in Tonga cante-
fable tradition.

This is different from the situation that arises
from instances of sexual births - the second major
mode of procreation in Tonga cante-fable tradition.
When a man marries only one wife, she usually gives
birth to a desired normal human baby, as may be seen
from narratives 34, 52, 53 and 74, to give only a few
examples; in one instance, 118, the only wife in a
monogamous marriage gives birth to a stone, but this
is exceptional.

In a polygamous situation where a man marries two
wives, however, one of the wives usually gives birth
to a wanted child, while the other wife bears a proscribed offspring. The criterion that determines
whether a child is wanted or not varies from one
situation to another. Generally, however, the criterion is either the sex or the multiplicity of the
offspring.

When sex is the criterion, the acceptable child is
always a son while the unwanted one is invariably a
girl, as is the case in Narrative No.21, for example.
On the other hand, when multiplicity of progeny is
the criterion, the wanted offspring results from a
single birth, while the proscribed one is inevitably
a set of twins, as in narrative No.7.

If the criterion is the sex of the progeny, the
tale is almost always about the banishment of the

unwanted daughter; in that case, she is the principal character of the narrative. On the other hand, when multiplicity of birth is the criterion, the tale generally centres around the banishment of the twins, who are the principal characters.

This is the nature of the building-block, Birth, in Tonga cante-fable tradition and it is from this reservoir of traditional lore that a narrator draws the form of Birth appropriate to the tale he narrates.

As mentioned earlier, Bynum defines theme as 'a conglomeration of narrative matter which recurs in the tradition, and which is discrete because some of its occurrences have no consistent sequential relationship with other such units.'

The building-block, Birth, is a conglomeration of narrative matter, which recurs twenty-seven times in my sample of Tonga cante-fable tradition. As may be seen in Chapter IV, it is discrete, since some of its occurrences have no consistent sequential relationship with other building-blocks in the seven multiforms of the story of the Banished Child. Thus, the role of this building-block is akin to that of a theme in an oral epic.

It is therefore tempting to call the building-block a theme of narrative No.7. Such a label is indeed justified because it has already been demonstrated in Chapter II that the Tonga tradition of cante-fable is an oral poetic one; themes, as defined by Lord,[10] exist only in oral poetic traditions. Consequently, one is right in applying Lord's model of thematic analysis to a study of Tonga cante-fable. Likewise, the other building-blocks in the Tonga tradition of cante-fable are the themes of this oral poetic tradition.

As has been demonstrated earlier, the tale of the Banished Child resembles a rite of passage, since its main action entails a separation, a transition and a reincorporation. Although there is nothing in the performance of Narrative No.7 or in the Tonga tradition of cante-fable to indicate that the tale is now part of a ritual, Van Gennep's model nevertheless provides a valuable framework for classifying the various themes encountered in the seven multiforms of this tale in my sample of the tradition. The themes

that lead up to the banishment of the twins to the
forest may be classified as the themes of Separation,
while those that pertain to the twins' sojourn in the
forest may be labelled the themes of Transition. In
the same manner, the themes that pertain to the reincorporation of the banished twins may be classified
as the themes of Reintegration.

CHAPTER IV

Themes of Separation

As has been demonstrated in Chapter III, the themes present in the tale of the Banished Child in my sample of the tradition may be classified into three categories: Separation, Transition, and Reintegration. This chapter deals with the first category, which in the sample is represented by the following eight themes: Birth, Marriage, Banishment, Protest, Neglect, Repudiation, Conception, and Journey. These eight themes belong together, because in the framework of the tale of the Banished Child, all of them take place at home and culminate in the banishment of the unwanted offspring. The theme of Birth has already been discussed, so I shall begin with the second of the series, that of Marriage.

Marriage

The marital pairs encountered in my collection are as follows: a man married to a woman; a man married to a wooden girl; a man married to a young girl who later turns herself into a zebra; a frog married to a chameleon; a man married to a female cannibal; a man married to a girl formed from congealed blood; animals married to human brides; an aquatic human being married to a girl; and a man married to a special girl who must not pound. These marital partners may be classified into three major groups: human, animal and anomalous marriages.

The human marriages in this tradition are strictly the marital affiliation of a man and a woman. It may be a monogamous arrangement, but it can also be a polygamous one; in which case a man may have two or more wives. This is in keeping with the situation in real Tonga society. It is remarkable, however, that although in reality a man can marry as many wives as he pleases, in the cante-fable tradition, the number of wives in a polygamous marriage is usually limited to two. So here again the cante-fable tradition rigidly restricts the options that are open to the male head of a polygamous household.

As was mentioned in my discussion of the theme of Birth, the number of wives in a household determines the range of possible offspring that may be born into the family. In the tradition, if a man is married to only one wife and she gives birth, the offspring may be a boy or a girl, but it will invariably be a single birth; twins are usually not born into a household where there is only one wife. In a polygamous family, however, the possibilities are much greater; one of the two wives can give birth to a single baby while the other bears a set of twins or one may give birth to a baby-girl while her co-wife bears a baby-boy. In a polygamous family the crucial factor is the maintenance of the balance between the two wives; hence, if one bears a baby of one sex, then the other must bear a baby of the opposite sex.

The animal marriages in the tradition are remarkable because of the degree of choice permitted the marital partners. Unlike the marriages between human spouses which are rigidly restricted by the tradition itself, the spouses in marriages between animals do not even have to belong to the same species. The Hare may marry the Elephant if he so desires. The only restriction noticeable in animal marriages in the cante-fable tradition is that they cannot give birth to human beings.

Anomalous marriages in this tradition are the ones in which one spouse may be human and the other not. In some instances of anomalous marriage, the bridegroom is a human being while the bride may be transformed blood or a log metamorphosed into a human being, as narrative No.57 shows. Here, although the bride is temporarily a human being, she is essentially a log; hence, she is eventually transformed back into her constituent wood. On the other hand, the bride may be an animal - usually a zebra - masquerading as a human being as is the case in No.61.

Not all anomalous marriages in the tradition consist of a human bridegroom and a non-human bride. There are instances where the bride is human while the bridegroom is the unnatural partner. Such is the case in narrative No.40 in which three animals disguised as men enter a human village and marry three girls left alone at home. Another example of the situation where the bridegroom is anomalous is narrative No.54 where two girls desperately want a ghost risen from the grave to marry them.

The anomalous marriages in the tradition are very intriguing because they create combinations of spouses that do not exist in real life. It is ironic, though, that despite the imaginative possibilities of this, the outcome is even more rigidly limited than the two other types of marriage in the tradition. The anomalous marriage is doomed to failure from the very start. Thus although the types of marriage possible in the cante-fables exceed those found in real life, one must not conclude that a story-teller is at liberty to use any type of marriage in whichever situation he pleases. The tradition restricts the options within each marital arrangement.

Banishment

In my collection, the use of this theme is restricted largely to the seven narratives about the Banished Child.

The narratives do not always give the reason why a child is banished. Even in those that offer some explanation, the reasons offered seem mere afterthoughts rather than convincing rationales. An example is narrative No.7, in which the young father says that he will not be able to sleep comfortably if he has to share his bed with the wife and her twin sons. Furthermore, he fears that the twins will dirty his house. These are trivial reasons for a father to banish his sons in real life, but they seem to suffice in the cante-fable tradition. In narrative No.46 one encounters another reason why another child - this time a girl - is banished from her home. Her father wants only boys to be born into his family because when the boys grow up they will be able to herd his cattle, and girls are useless since they cannot perform such a duty. These are the two most common reasons found in the narratives as to why twin boys and girls are banished.

The tradition limits the possible places to which these children may be banished. Usually the father

wants them to be thrown out and left to die, but very
often the mother of the children takes them to a
forest or to a cave. There, either an old woman or a
spirit adopts and provides for them till they grow
up.

As has already been mentioned, in some instances of
banishment - No.7 for instance - the natural mother
may regularly feed her banished children on ordinary
food which she brings to them from her home. Elsewhere, the child thrives on the wild food which her
foster-parent procures from the forest.

In most cases, the banishment comes to an end
during the adolescence of the rejected children.
Usually the banishment is terminated by the father's
going into the forest, being reconciled to his banished children, and taking them back to the village.
This is the normal scenario. What usually varies
from one account to another is the father's reason
for going into the forest in the first place. He may
go to kill the suspected lover of his wife (as in
narrative No.7). Or, as in narrative No.46, he goes
there because someone who has seen his daughter takes
him there to meet her. Here, unlike the situation in
No.7, the father knows very well what to expect from
his journey into the forest.

Consequently, the theme consists of the following
elements: the reason; the place; the duration; and
the motivation for the father's journey which terminates the banishment.

Protest

Protests in Tonga tradition of cante-fable sometimes result from the repudiation of one's responsibility to one's Kinsmen. An instance is narrative
No.7, where the husband repudiates the wife who bears
him twin sons. The wife protests against the husband's decision, but this - like other protests under
similar circumstances in the tradition - is to no
avail. Another example of this is in narrative No.23.

A bride's first journey to the home of her new
spouse is another situation that often generates protests. The new bride is usually accompanied by a
younger brother who refuses to go home when asked to

do so. Angered by the boy's intransigence, the new bride in such situations often beats her younger kinsman in order to force him to return home. Usually it is not the younger who protests; it is rather the elder sister's companions who protest on his behalf, and unlike the ineffectual protests about repudiation which I have already discussed, the protests of the elder sister's companions achieve their objective. Ironically, it is the young boy who finally rescues the bride and her companions from husbands who invariably turn out to be animals, as in narrative No.25.

Another situation that generates efficacious protest is represented in narrative No.26. Here the animals compete as to which of them is to marry the most beautiful girl in the village. Such a belle often feigns to be dumb, and the task of the suitors is to make her talk; whoever succeeds in this will be her husband. As is usual in such a situation, the big animals like the Elephant and the Lion propose to her first without success, but the cunning little Hare succeeds by cutting down the girl's maize and forcing her to protest against his action. The girl's protest normally halts the Hare's action, but it also gives him a wife.

Sometimes the protest arises from a situation in which a bride is set a task which she considers demeaning. In some instances - No.73 for example - the bride is an old wife, but in many others (Nos.49 and 63 for instance), the bride is newly wed. In No.73 the hunter's old wife protests without success against her husband's instruction to cook delicious meals for his dog. When she finally decides to feed the dog what she considers to be appropriate dog food, the dog becomes angry and bites off her breast. Narrative No.49 centres around a problem of mistaken identity: the new bridegroom mistakes his new bride's slave-girl for the bride and treats his bride as if she were a slave-girl. Like the protest in narrative No.73, the bride's protest here is without success. The same is true of the protest of the bride in No.63.

The kidnapping of someone's wife or daughter is yet another situation which generates protest in Tonga cante-fable tradition, as is exemplified in narratives 50 and 89. Here again the protest is of no avail.

In conclusion, protests in this tradition generally arise from marriage situations. Although there are instances of efficacious protests, most often protests have no effect.

Neglect

A situation that usually generates Neglect arises when a wife must cater for the needs of her dead co-wife's living child. In such situations the living wife usually neglects her obligations to the dead woman's child - most often a girl - as in narrative No.1. In such situations, the wife often takes good care of her own daughters but converts the orphan into a servant. This is the situation in No.1 as well as in No.68A. In these cases, however, the dead mother comes to the aid of her maltreated daughter. In No.1 the dead mother appears to her daughter in the guise of a soul-bird, and bedecks her daughter with the finery that helps her attract the attention of the prince who later marries her. In 68A, the mother emerges from the river, looking exactly like her former self, breast-feeds her infant daughter, and helps the adolescent one carry her heavy pot of water.

Neglect of young children is not limited, however, to wicked step-mothers. There are instances, as in narratives 7 and 18, in which a mother neglects to feed her own children. The difference between a mother's neglect and that of a foster-mother is that there is no malice involved when a biological mother neglects her children. In narrative No.7 for instance, the mother fails to feed her children because it is inconvenient for her and she feels that they can feed themselves with the left-overs from a previous meal.

Sometimes, it is the male head of a household who neglects to care for his family, as we see in narrative No.90. Here, the head of the family is drunk and quarrelsome most of the time and often neglects to provide food for his family.

Sometimes the object of the neglect is not a human being but an animal, as in narratives 16 and 50. In such situations, it is usually a woman who neglects to feed the animal left under her care. This is invariably the animal that guards the women; hence, when it is too famished to protect her, the woman's enemies are able to carry her away.

Thus, there are two major types of neglect discernible in my sample of tales. The first is the neglect of a person, usually by a kinsman, while the second is the neglect of a custodial animal - usually by the woman whom it protects.

Repudiation

This theme is akin to that of Neglect except that the theme of Repudiation usually involves the formal separation of man and wife; hence it also entails the renunciation of obligation to a spouse.

In this tradition it is often the husband who repudiates his wife, especially when she gives birth to an unwanted child. As mentioned in the discussion of the theme of Birth, there are many reasons why a father may not want a particular child. If the father wants sons to herd cattle, for example, a girl born to the family becomes an unwanted child, and the father may repudiate her mother on this account. This is exemplified in narrative No.21.

At other times, however, the husband may want only one child to be born, so that twins become unwanted children, as in narratives Nos. 7 and 18.

It is remarkable that instances in which a man repudiates his wife occur only in polygamous families. This is another instance of the tradition narrowing the options available in any given situation. In cases where a husband repudiates one wife, he usually makes the other one his preferred wife. Again, once the husband is reconciled to the unwanted child(ren) and mother, he invariably repudiates his previously preferred wife and her child, thus completing the cycle of repudiation. This is what happens in narratives 7, 18 and 46.

In this tradition, it is not only the husbands who can repudiate their wives. There are examples in my

sample of tales where the wives repudiate their husbands, but these are not as common as husbands'
repudiations of wives. This is a slight modification
of the situation in real life; in Tonga society,
women repudiate their husbands more often than the
other way round. In that sense, then, the situation
that emerges from the cante-fable tradition is an
idealisation of real Tonga marriage.

In the cases where the wife repudiates her husband,
she does so only after her husband has grossly maltreated her - usually after fist-fights - as in
narratives No.29 and 90. In No.90, the wife repudiates her husband because he is constantly drunk,
often fights with her and is incapable of providing
for his family.

It would thus appear that the wives in real Tonga
are freer to repudiate their husbands than the ones
portrayed in the tales. Women in real Tonga society
- as well as other societies - are known to desert
their husbands simply because they have found other
lovers. By limiting the freedom of action of the
wives in the cante-fables, the tradition indeed
romanticizes the fidelity of Tonga women.

Conception

Conception is used here to denote the period of
gestation rather than the moment of fertilization.
Narrators in this tradition are unlikely to discuss
the nature of the conception, but only the progeny
born later. One must therefore deduce the nature of
the conception by working backwards from the available information about the nature of the progeny.

Based on the information deduced from my sample of
tales, there are several modes of conception in the
Tonga tradition of cante-fable. Some are those of
animals which bear their young, like the Hare in
narrative No.5. Others are those of birds which
incubate their eggs, like the guinea-fowl in narrative No.15. In this tradition, however, it is quite
possible for a human being to help incubate the eggs
laid by a bird, as narrative No.15 demonstrates.

Most often the conceptions are those of human
beings. In a monogamous marriage the wife can

89

conceive several times, depending on the number of children the narrative necessitates. In a polygamous marriage, the two wives invariably conceive at the same time, but the kind of babies they conceive depends on the plot of the narrative. In narratives about Banished Children, for instance, one wife has to conceive a wanted child while the other must conceive an unwanted child or children.

There is a special mode of conception that appears from time to time in the tradition. This is the asexual conception that takes place in a pot or a jar, as is manifested in narrative No.11. As previously mentioned, these situations in which a woman's non-menstrual blood transforms itself into a child after some period of gestation are symbolic representations of the normal human conception.

What is remarkable in the Conception theme in this tradition is that although human beings and animals can intermarry no conceptions occur; hence, no births ever result from such unions.

Journey

The theme of Journey occurs quite frequently in Tonga cante-fable tradition - certainly more frequently than any other theme in the story of the Banished Child. The purpose of a journey is a criterion for classifying the various incidences of the theme that occur in my sample.

In Tonga cante-fable tradition, a journey may be made for the sole purpose of procuring a bride (as in narratives: 20, 26, 39, 40, 53, 55, 61, 63, 76, 81, 93, and 95). Such a journey normally comprises three parts: the outward journey; the bridal journey; and the bridal return. The first is a man's first journey to the home of his future wife, while the second is the bride's first journey to the home of her husband. The third is the bride's flight from the husband's home. Not all the journeys in this category have all the three parts listed above, and sometimes a narrative may have only the bridal journey without its two other complements.

The details of the outward journey may vary from one narrative to another. Essentially, however, it is one

which a man makes to the home of his proposed bride,
and he may be accompanied on this journey by other
suitors, as in narrative No.40, where three prospective husbands travel together, but more often than
not a suitor is unaccompanied, as in No.20 where a
day-old *enfant terrible* sets out all by himself to
procure a bride. Although the unaccompanied suitor
is more frequent in the tradition, he often belongs
to a group whose members compete to find out who
among them will win the hand of the beautiful girl,
as in narrative No.26. In this tradition, only men
undertake this kind of outward journey.

The bridal journey is a bride's first visit to the
home of her new husband, and the composition of the
party which sets out on such a journey is different
from that of the one which makes the outward journey.
The bride is the most important member of the party,
and she is usually accompanied - often against her
will - by her younger brother, the bridegroom and his
companions, as in narrative No.40. But she may be
accompanied only by another girl, as narrative No.49
illustrates. The bridal return is usually the
bride's flight from the home of her husband on
account of some marital discord. In some narratives
the bride returns to her parents because her husband
turns out to be an animal (as in No.40) but elsewhere
she returns home to her parents because her husband
and his people maltreat her (as in narratives 63 and
49).

Another type of journey whose purpose is the procurement of a bride is the one aimed at the kidnapping of a woman. The woman may be someone else's
wife (as in narratives 57 and 19) or someone's
daughter (as in narrative No.50). It is remarkable
that in all the incidences of women abducted, the
abductors do not achieve their ultimate goal. They
usually manage to take the woman to their own home,
but they cannot keep her long, since the woman's
husband or father follows them and thwarts their
desires by taking her back home or transforming her
into her original element.

Sometimes the purpose of the journey is to seek a
proper burial place in which to dispose of the
remains of a loved one, as in No.52, where a young

91

boy seeks a river wherein to cast the remains of his mother. At other times, however, the purpose may be to find a means of reviving dead relatives (as in Nos. 43, 85 and 86). In No.43, for instance, the mother who loses all her ten children journeys to the land of the dead in search of them. As often happens in such situations, she achieves her objective and brings them back to the land of the living.

Sometimes the purpose of the journey is to acquire wealth (as in narrative No.92) where a group of young men journey to a distant town to buy valuable hoes. At other times the purpose of the journey is to cultivate a piece of land, as in narrative Nos. 80 and 97. Sometimes people make a journey into the forest in order to procure wild fruit (as in narrative No.45), or go there in order to hunt wild animals with which to feed their wives (as in narrative No.57). At other times, however, they go into the forest in order to look for honey (as in No.57). Sometimes a mother journeys to the forest in order to shelter her Banished Children in a rock cave, or she goes there to feed them, and she usually journeys there in search of them if she imagines that they are lost (as in narrative No.7).

Quite often a man and his wife journey to his wife's home to visit her relatives (as in narrative No.94). This kind of journey is different from the bridal return which has already been discussed, and is not indicative of marital discord.

There are some journeys a woman can undertake without danger to herself. She may go to be cicatrised or to have her front teeth pulled out in ancient Tonga fashion (as in narrative No.24). But she must not go to fish in a pond by a dam (as in narrative No.25). She must not go into the forest in search of her husband who is hunting (as In No.6), nor follow him to collect wild fruit (as in narrative No.68B), for she is likely to be attacked on such occasions by a large monster-bird. She may even be abandoned in the top of a tree.

Sometimes people make a journey to a distant place, like Johannesburg, in order to seek wage-paying employment (as in narrative No.39). But as in real Tonga society, such journeys are restricted to adolescent men and women do not undertake them.

From the discussion above, one may conclude that there are many multiforms of the theme of Journey in this cante-fable tradition. However, the tradition limits what can happen to the travellers in each type of Journey. For example, only two things can happen to a suitor who goes to the home of his prospective bride. He may find that his future bride is alone in the house, or he may meet his would-be parents-in-law when he arrives. If the bride is alone, the suitor may take her to his home without her parents' consent. Such a situation portends danger either for the bride, as in narrative No.40 where the suitors later turn out to be Lions disguised as human beings, or for the suitor, as in narrative No.93 where the father-in-law eventually kills his son-in-law for having earlier eloped with his daughter. If on the other hand the suitor meets his prospective parents-in-law when he arrives, they often subject him to a series of tests. Narrative No.20 is an instance of this. Here the suitor is made to eat poisoned food, bathe in water that kills anyone it touches, and climb a gigantic palm-tree before he is allowed to take his bride home.

Again what can happen to a woman who goes into a forest or to a dam is strictly limited by the tradition. If she goes into the forest in order to secure a place of refuge for her Banished Child, nothing evil happens to her. But if she goes there in search of her husband, for instance, a monster-bird invariably ambushes her, as in narrative No.6. In addition, the tradition also restricts the events that can take place when a living person goes to the land of the dead. Such a traveller often meets an old woman who subjects him to a test, as in narrative No.43. Here, the old woman tests the traveller by asking her to eat maggots and it is only afterwards that she shows the mother the way leading to the land of the dead.

CHAPTER V

Themes of Transition

This chapter deals with the second category of
themes. In the present sample of the tradition, this
is represented by nineteen themes: Adolescence,
Instruction, Purification, Lament, Transformation,
Search, Donation, Contest, Attack, Adoption, Revelation, Loss, Deception, Reassurance, Jealousy, Doubt,
Defeat, Recovery, and Recognition.

The themes listed above belong together, because in
the framework of the tale of the Banished Child they
all take place in the forest - transitional abode and
a place of refuge which is betwixt and between the
banishment of the unwanted offspring and the reintegration of these same children into the society that
rejected them initially. What follows is a description of the themes of transition.

Adolescence

In real Tonga society, adolescence is a stage in
one's development which begins in late childhood and
terminates when one gets married. During this phase,
which spans many years, one is considered a young
adult. It is in the same manner that the theme of
Adolescence is used in the cante-fable tradition.

Judging from the episodes in the tradition, one can
deduce that adolescence is regarded by the Tonga as a
period of life when one can engage in various kinds
of activities. It is the time when girls go to be
cicatrised as in narrative No.15, as well as to have
their front teeth removed - an ancient Tonga cosmetic
custom - as exemplified in narrative No.24. Adolescence appears in the Tonga tradition of cante-fable
as a period when the persons involved acquire the
culture of their society. The process of acquisition,
however, does not have to take place within the con-
fines of the human village; it may also take place in
the forest, as often happens with banished children.
As is to be expected in such situations, what the

young person learns from the experience of living in the forest may often differ from the culture of his native village. Narrative No.7 gives evidence of this. Here the twin boys banished into the forest are endowed with a mansion by their foster-father and there they drink tea. The mansion and the tea, in the context of the tale, are alien to the culture of the twins' native village, as is the sophistication which they teach their mother when she visits them, especially the art of using facial cosmetics.

Being exiled is not the only misfortune that can befall a young adult in the cante-fable tradition. Adolescent girls whose mothers have died are often subjected to oppressive servitude by their fathers' other wives, as is exemplified in narrative No.1. For those who are not subjected to these misfortunes, adolescence can be a period of exciting and sometimes dangerous adventures, as seen in narrative No.25, where the girls endanger their lives by fishing in the forbidden dam-pond. It is also not unusual for such adolescent girls to set out for the homes of the men who propose to marry them without first informing their parents, as in narratives 40, 54, 55 and 76. Such behaviour, however, hardly ever happens in real Tonga society. Even in the cante-fable tradition itself, the results of such hurriedly-arranged marriages are rigidly limited. Most of the options open to other married couples are closed to them; their marriage is doomed to failure from the very beginning because the bridegrooms turn out to be either ghosts, as in narrative No.54, or lions as in Nos. 40, 55 and 76.

The exciting adolescent adventures found in the tradition are not restricted to girls; adolescent boys enjoy such adventures too. Adolescence is often the time when young men travel to distant lands in order to make a fortune for themselves, either by wage earning (as in narratives No.37 and 39) or by purchasing treasured objects which they hope to sell at a profit back in their own villages (as in narrative No.92). Adolescent boys can be quite reckless, like the boy in No.36, who allowed his father's snake to escape, but they can be responsible, especially when it comes to herding the family cattle, as narrative No.44 demonstrates. Indeed it is not unusual for adolescent boys to begin to provide for the members of their family, particularly after the death of their parents, as in No.60 and in No.52, where an adolescent boy undertakes to give his dead mother a special burial in a river rather than on land.

Judging from the numerous examples in which adolescence culminates in marriage, it appears that the principal goal of adolescence in this cante-fable tradition is to prepare the young adults for marriage. This is in keeping with the norms of real Tonga society in which marriage is the most important rite of passage that transforms young adults into responsible members of society. Adolescence indeed is a transitional period between the carefree life of infants and the responsibilities of being a married adult. It is a period during which young people acquire the culture of their society.

Instruction

The object of instruction has varied forms in Tonga cante-fable tradition. Sometimes the object of instruction pertains ostensibly to personal hygiene, as in narrative No.1, where the mother of a destitute girl instructs her to bathe in a small pond hidden under the grass. This is similar to the situation in narrative No.7, in which twin boys instruct their mother to take a bath. In such situations more is entailed than mere acts of physical cleanliness, for the bathing is a purificatory act, and the instruction given here concerns ritual purity. The recipient of the instruction in each case carries it out, and thus is prepared for the next phase of a spiritual journey - one of spiritual Transformation - which is yet another theme encountered in the tale of the Banished Child.

Sometimes the instruction pertains to one's role as a member of a family. In narrative No.7, when the mother of the Banished Twins visits them in the forest, the twin boys instruct her to behave well towards their father regardless of whatever he may do to her. When she returns to the village, she begins

to play the role her children played while she was in
the forest, and she instructs her husband not to
expel her co-wife. It may also pertain to the care
of animals left in one's charge, as seen in narratives 16 and 50. In each case a man who is about to
go on a long journey leaves an animal - a cock in
No.16 and a dog in No.50 - to guard his female kin
at home. In each case too he instructs his kinswoman
- wife in No.16 and daughter in No.50 - to feed the
animal left in her care. In such situations, however, the woman after a while ignores the instruction,
and is usually abducted when the animal is too weak
to defend her. Occasionally the instruction pertains
to the means of escape from a dangerous predicament,
as exemplified in narratives 15 and 25. Here a young
girl overhears an old witch perform the rites which
open the gates to her home, and later instructs her
elder sisters how to sing the incantatory song which
enables them to escape from captivity. No.25 is
another multiform of this. Here an old woman who
lives in the forest instructs a young boy to construct a drum which later transports him with his
elder sister and her companions to safety.

The instruction may pertain to a means of avenging
a wrong. This is illustrated by narrative No.23,
where a herbalist instructs an old woman to abandon
her young daughter-in-law in a tree in order to
avenge her daughter-in law's neglect. It may also
pertain to a means of identification, as in narrative
No.28, where Elephant teaches his wife a song, which
is a code enabling her to identify him when he comes
home from a hunting trip. In this tradition, however, such instruction works against the instructor,
for an enemy invariably intercepts the code and uses
it to gain entrance to the house, when he either
abducts the residents, as in narrative No.28, or
kills them, as in No.83.

Finally, instruction pertains to ways to achieve a
desired goal. In narrative No.43 a woman searches
for the way to the land of the dead in order to rescue her dead children, while in No.52 a young boy
needs to be instructed as to the right path to a
certain river-bank, where he plans to bury his
mother. If the instruction is followed in such

situations, the objective will be achieved, but if
rejected the end may be tragic, as in the case of the
jealous co-wife of narrative No.43, who disregards
the instructions of the old woman she meets in the
land of the dead.

Thus there are various needs for instruction, and
many people give it in Tonga cante-fable tradition.
It is not only the old who instruct the young; the
young may also instruct their elders. It would also
appear that by complying with instruction, one is
more likely to achieve an objective.

Purification

There are three modes of Purification: the first
is by water, the second by sweeping with a broom, and
the third by fire.

Narrative No.1 provides an example of Purification
by water. In this tale a girl, acting on the advice
of her mother, bathes in a nearby stream, and thereby
becomes as clean as a girl who has just left her
puberty enclosure. Here the girl's physical cleanliness is symbolic of her inner purity; hence the
cleansing with water is a purificatory act. People's
clothes can also be cleansed with water, as in narrative No.7, where the twins wash the clothes which
their mother brought with her from the village.
Already purified herself and bedecked in fine clothes,
the transformed mother stands in great contrast to
her old clothes; hence, the need for these to be
purified too.

Narrative No.46 provides the only example of the
second mode - purification by sweeping. Here a man
sweeps his compound clean of all rubbish prior to
welcoming back his banished daughter. The act of
sweeping with a broom is a symbolic representation of
the rescinding of his unjust prohibition of the birth
of girls in his family.

Narrative No.7 exemplifies the third mode of
Purification. Here the man who banished his twin
sons burns his old blanket when his wife gives him a
new one she received from her banished sons. The
fire which burns the dirty blanket is symbolic of the
later cleansing of the man's home of the ritual

impurity he introduced into it by his unjust banishment of his twin sons.

As may be seen in narratives: 17, 21, 40, 60, 7,
46, 47, 49, 20, 79, 82 and 118, the three modes of
Purification resemble a rite of passage which a person undergoes when he or she is at the threshold of
a new career in life. As van Gennep suggests in
Rites of Passage[11], such rituals regenerate the
individuals involved and inbue them with the strength
they need to cope with what lies ahead. This is
especially applicable to narrative No.49, where a
bride suddenly finds herself being treated as a slave
girl, while her slave girl is treated as if she were
a bride. Whenever the bride wearies of her unaccus-
tomed backbreaking tasks, she sings and the rains
fall, thereby purifying and invigorating her. This
is also true of narrative No.21, as whenever the
banished girl is depressed she sings and the rains
fall and cleanse her.

Sometimes the purificatory act functions as a test
of humility. Such is the case in narratives: 43 and
52. In No.43 an old woman who lives in the land of
the dead asks a mother who is seeking a way to revive her dead children to bathe her. Although it is
not so stated in this particular narrative, the old
woman's body in such a situation is usually covered
by festering ulcers. The test is therefore to find
out whether the mother will do the thing natural for
one from the land of the living, which is to refuse
to touch the old woman and her stinking ulcers, or
whether, on the other hand, she will be humble enough
to do what she is asked. In this example, the first
mother passes the test, while the second one does the
'natural' thing and so fails the test.

Sometimes the act of purification is used as an
insurmountable obstacle, as manifested in narrative
No.59. Here the crafty Tortoise insists that the
Baboon wash his hands in a nearby river before sit-
ting down to drink with him. But the Tortoise has
burnt a patch of grass outside his house; thus the
Baboon's hands become soiled each time just before he
enters the Tortoise's house. After washing and
soiling his hands a couple of times, the Baboon realises that the Tortoise has set him an impossible task

and meekly watches the Tortoise drink all the wine by
himself.

Thus the three modes of purification are alike in
many respects. Apart from the few instances where
the act of purification is used as a trick, all three
have ritual significance.

Lament

Laments are very often connected with deep personal
loss, either of a beloved relative, as in narrative
No.7, where a mother laments the loss of her twin
sons, or of a treasured object, as in No.39, where a
young man laments the loss of the magical ring which
provides him with everything his heart desires.
Laments may also be associated with regret, and dis-
satisfaction with the predicament in which one finds
oneself, as in narrative No.61. Here the Zebra who
disguised herself as a human bride laments her marriage to a real human being.

Narrators in the tradition have two methods of
handling laments in their narratives. They may simply indicate, as in narrative No.7, that the mother
of the twins laments the loss of her children. Or
they may dwell on the lament in detail, and then
invariably present the lament in the form of a song.
This is demonstrated in narrative No.43, where the
mother whose ten children have all died sings her
lament while she is on her way to bring them back
from the land of the dead. The fictitious singers of
the lament songs are usually those who themselves are
bereaved. The content of the songs varies from one
situation to another; the content of each lament must
suit the situation at hand. This is exemplified by
the two following laments from my collection:

I

You, Cinyinza, my brother-in-law
Cinyinza, Cinyinza, my brother-in-law

You, Cinyinza, my brother-in-law
Cinyinza, Cinyinza, my brother-in-law

You are sleeping. You do not take me to my home
Cinyinza, Cinyinza, my brother-in-law

You are sleeping. You do not take me to my home
Cinyinza, Cinyinza, my brother-in-law.

At my home where we eat meat
Cinyinza, Cinyinza, my brother-in-law

You are sleeping nzyii nzyii nzyii
Cinyinza, Cinyinza my brother-in-law

You, Cinyinza, my brother-in-law
Cinyinza, Cinyinza, my brother-in-law

You, Cinyinza, my brother-in-law
Cinyinza, Cinyinza, my brother-in-law

You are sleeping. You do not take me to my home
Cinyinza, Cinyinza, my brother-in-law

You are sleeping. You do not take me to my home
Cinyinza, Cinyinza, my brother-in-law

At my home where we eat meat
Cinyinza, Cinyinza, my brother-in-law

You are sleeping nzyii nzyii nzyii
Cinyinza, Cinyinza, my brother-in-law

You are sleeping nzyii nzyii nzyii
Cinyinza, Cinyinza, my brother-in-law

II

Ngoma, your stick hurts me
Do not worry. Do not worry

At your home boys herd cattle
Do not worry. Do not worry

Ngoma, your stick hurts me
Do not worry. Do not worry.

Ngoma, your stick hurts me
Do not worry. Do not worry.

In the first of these two laments (from narrative
No.61) the animal bride laments her fateful marriage
to a real human being, while in the second (taken

from No.56) an adolescent girl protests against her
banishment from her home where only boys are considered good enough to herd cattle. Thus in this
tradition, anyone - human being or animal - is permitted to sing a lament, but the content of the
lament must be appropriate to each situation.

Transformation

There are numerous modes of Transformation in Tonga
cante-fable tradition, but by far the most common is
a transformation from one state of being to another
and is exemplified in narratives: 1, 11, 19, 37, 40,
44, 47, 55, 57, 60, 61, 63, 75, 76, 81, 89, 92, 93
and 95. These may be subdivided into nine subgroups.
  In the first subgroup (represented by narrative
No.19) a log of wood is transformed into a woman and
married by someone who later re-transforms her back
into wood. The second subgroup entails the transformation of a human being into an animal, and is
exemplified by narrative No.37: a man transforms
himself into a lion in order to kill his son, but is
himself killed in the process. The third subgroup is
an inversion of the second, and entails the transformation of an animal into a human being, as in
narrative No.40: a group of animals transform themselves into human beings and set out to marry human
brides, later transforming themselves back into animals in order to eat their brides. The fourth is the
transformation of wood into wealth, as in narrative
No.44, and thus has something in common with the
first subgroup, as wood is transformed into another
element. The fifth entails the transformation of a
fish into a human being and so is a multiform of the
third subgroup; it is exemplified by narrative No.47,
where a fish transforms itself into a girl and later
back into a fish. The sixth is the transformation of
the spirit of a dead person into a soul-bird, as in
narrative No.60, where a young man killed by his
companions transforms himself into a soul-bird and
exposes his murderers. The seventh entails the
transformation of a human being into a vegetable, as
in narrative No.63, where the new bride is transformed into a pumpkin plant and is later

re-transformed into a human being by her younger
brother. The eighth is the transformation of blood
into a human being as in narrative No.75. Here an
old woman's leached blood transforms itself into a
girl who is subsequently kidnapped by the old woman's
jealous neighbours. Angered by the kidnappers'
action, the old woman re-transforms the girl into her
component blood.

Transformation from life to death is the ninth subgroup. Narrators do not always indicate what is the
cause of death, but one may deduce that physical
exhaustion resulting from the overtaxing of stamina
is one possible cause, as in narrative No.22. Starvation, especially during a famine, is often another
cause of death, as in narrative 45. The high incidence of famine in Tonga cante-fable reflects the
society's real dependence on the vagaries of the
annual rains, as in other rural agricultural communi-
ties in areas of marginal rainfall. In a good year
when there is ample rainfall there is bountiful
harvest, but a year of scanty or no rains is often a
prelude to a long period of famine which in turn
generates mass starvation and death, as in narrative
No.45.

Water can also be an agency of death in this tradition. Someone may die by drowning, and often the
river is not merely a passive recipient of the body
that has fallen into it. On the contrary, the river
may be portrayed as having grabbed the drowned person,
especially when he or she has committed an offence
beforehand, as in narrative No.87. Here the river
drowns the girl who steals some of the fruit that
belongs to her friends, but does not want to admit it;
in this narrative the river plays the role of the
malefactor's executioner. Sometimes water may also
kill a person who has not even fallen into it; water
in a bowl can kill someone who looks into it, as may
be seen from narrative No.93, in which Mazumba dies
from looking into a bowl of water offered to him by
his father-in-law. Thus water is a potent cause of
death in this cante-fable tradition.

Murder is another agency of death (transformation).
In the Tonga tradition, the murdered and victim
often have kinship ties, being related by birth or

through marriage. When by birth, they may relate to
each other in most of the possible permutations of
affinal relationships one finds in real life. The
murderer may be a son while the victim is his father,
or vice versa, as in narrative No.37. Both the
assailant and the victim may also be brothers, as in
narrative No.60. The assailant may be a mother while
the victim is her daughter, as in narratives 11 and
75, or the murderer may be a son and his victims his
own mother, brothers, and sisters, as in narrative
No.95. When the victims and the assailant are related through marriage the tradition again permits them
to relate to one another in most of the possible permutations of marital relationships one finds in real
life. The assailant is often a husband and the
victim his wife, as in narratives Nos. 57 and 89; but
it may be the other way round, as in narrative No.94.
The assailant and the victims may be co-wives in a
polygamous marriage, as in narrative No.68A, but the
murderer may also be a parent-in-law while the victim
is a daughter-in-law, as in narrative No.63; the
reverse is the case in narrative No.95. The victim
may be a prospective son-in-law while the assailant
is his would-be father-in-law, as in narrative No.20.
The prospective murderer may also be a future mother-
in-law, as in narrative No.118. The intended victim
- in this case a prospective son-in-law - can murder
his would-be murderer and mother-in-law, as in narrative No.118. The assailant and the victim do not,
however, need to have any ties of kinship or marriage,
and may be no more than mere companions, as in narratives 13 and 92. Indeed they need not even know one
another, as in narrative No.50, where a father kills
the abductors of his daughter. In this case it is
plausible to assume that the father has never even
met these abductors before.

Death as portrayed in this tradition, however, is
merely a rite of passage which transforms the victim
from one state of being to another. There is no
finality about it; the dead can transform themselves
into soul-birds and ghosts in order to visit their
living kinsmen, as in narrative No.1. In certain
cases, the dead can transform themselves back into
living people, as in narrative No.43, where a mother

whose ten children die journeys to the land of the
dead and brings them back to her home. This, in
effect, involves a double transformation - first from
life to death and then from death to life.

Although transformation from one state of being to
another is by far the most common, it is not the only
mode of transformation. Transformation of wearing
apparel is quite important in the tradition too, and
usually entails the replacement of one's old, dirty
and often tattered clothes with clean, new ones (as
in narratives 1, 7, 79, etc.). In narrative No.7,
for instance, the twins bedeck their mother with new
clothes to replace the old ones she brought from her
husband's village. Another kind of transformation
involves the change from a state of uncleanness to
one of cleanliness, as in narratives 7 and 21. This
is usually preceded by an ablution, either in a bath
(as in No.7) or by rain water (as in No.21). Yet
another kind of transformation involves that of place,
as happens in No.39, when a magical ring transforms a
forest into a village with many beautiful houses, but
this mode is not very common in the tradition.

Not all transformations are as spectacular as the
above. Some entail only the transformation of size,
from small to large, as in narrative No.23, where a
mother-in-law transforms a normal tree into a gigantic one and in this way traps her daughter-in-law on
top of it. The transformation may also entail a
diminution in size, as in narrative No.40 where a
young boy puts his elder sister and her companions
into a drum and so helps them to escape death at the
hands of their animal husbands.

Sometimes the transformation is one of condition,
from good health to ill health and vice versa. This
is not very common, and appears only twice in my
sample of tales, in narratives 82 and 88. In No.82,
a snake which only young boys are capable of bringing
home manages to restore a sick old man to good health.
In No.88, however, the toad which a lame man mali-
ciously feeds to his blind friend transforms the
blind man into one with good eye-sight. In turn the
beatings of the outraged man who had been blind cures
his lame friend and transforms his crippled legs into
strong and healthy ones.

Yet another kind of transformation discernible in the tradition is the transformation of roles. This happens when a new bride arrives at the home of her new husband, particularly in cases where the bride has been pampered in her parent's home and may even have had a slave-girl ministering to her needs. For such brides, marriage usually brings a change in roles, since they now have to perform tasks they would have loathed in their parental homes. Examples of this are in narratives 52 and 63.

Thus it can be seen that there are many categories of the theme of transformation encountered in this tradition of cante-fables. Although the purpose of the transformation varies, each entails a change from one mode of existence to another.

Search

The theme of Search in the Tonga tradition of cante-fable is often closely linked to that of Loss, but is a separate theme, because the two do not always appear one after the other.

As to the purpose of the search, one can discern three types; search for a person, a place, and an object. Within each of these three categories, the specific goal of the search may vary from one situation to another. For example, within the category of the search for a person, the goal may be to locate a husband who has gone out to hunt, as in narrative No.6. Here a wife foolishly goes into the forest in search of her husband, despite good advice from her co-wife, but does not find him; instead she encounters a large monster bird which devours her children. Sometimes, the goal of the search is to locate a banished kinsman - frequently a child who has been adopted by a supernatural being in the forest (as in narrative No.7). In such instances, the first search is usually fruitless, but in subsequent searches the mother generally finds her children in a state preferable to their previous one, as in No.7, where they are ensconced in a mansion, when she left them earlier in a cave. At other times, the goal is to locate an abducted kinsman - usually a wife or child. The outcome is predictably the same in the two situations of abduction, because when the person conducting the search finds the kidnapped relative, he or she invariably metamorphoses the lost one. This is exemplified in narrative No.11, where the mother of a kidnapped girl comes home and does not find her daughter, sets out for the village of her daughter's abductors, and when she finds her child, pulls off the daughter's life-centre; in this manner, she transforms her back into her constituent blood. The same is the case in No.57, the only difference being that here it is a husband who pulls off the life-centre of his wife and in this way transforms her back to her component wood. In this cante-fable tradition, this is the invariable end of the search for a kidnapped kinsman when the lost one is an unnatural person.

The conclusion of the search for such unnatural kinsmen stands in remarkable contrast to that for kidnapped kinsmen who are normal human beings, as shown in narrative No.50. Here a father finally finds his abducted daughter at the home of her kidnappers, but does not kill her. Instead he kills as many of her abductors as he can and returns home with his daughter.

There are different forms of the second type of search - the search for a place - in the tradition also. In this group, the search for a home of the dead is most prominent. The goal of this varies; in some tales the objective is to locate the approximate place of repose for one's dead kinsman, as in No.52, where a young boy searches for a river in which to bury the remains of his dead mother, and through the assistance of some other-world persons, manages to bring home much wealth from his journey. Sometimes the goal is to revive one's dead kinsmen, as in narrative No.43. In such situations, with the assistance of old women who inhabit the other world, the human searchers usually succeed in finding the dead kinsmen and in bringing them home to the land of the living.

The third category of search - the search for an object - may also take many forms. The goal of a particular search in this category may be to procure a snake which can cure an old sick kinsman, as in

narrative 82, or it may also be to procure a magical
ring stolen by an unfaithful wife as in narrative
No.39. Thus although the purpose and result of the
search may vary from one situation to another, there
are three basic types of search in the tradition -
for a person, a place, or an object.

Donation

Based on the evidence of my sample of tales, there
are two major multiforms of the theme of Donation in
this tradition, the donation of provision, and the
donation of nourishment. In the first the recipient
is given objects of his material culture, and in the
second items of food.

The first type of donation - provision - manifests
itself in many forms. It may take the form of the
tree-bark which the mother of the twin boys in narrative No.7 prepares to serve as blankets for her banished children, or it may be the shelter which the
spirit with one eye, one hand, and one leg in the
same narrative provides for the twins later in his
forest mansion. It may be in the form of the simple
axe which the benevolent old woman of the forest
gives to a young boy to enable him construct a drum
to transport him and his companions to safety, as in
narrative No.25, or a magical ring which a master
gives to a faithful servant about to return permanently to his native village, in narrative No.39; the
ring furnishes the servant with a car, fine clothes,
and whatever else he desires. It may be a means of
escape, like the drum by which the young boy in
narratives 25, 40, and 76 rescues his elder sister
and her friends from the menacing animals intent on
eating them. It may also be utilitarian, like the
dog a father provides for his dauther's protection in
narrative No.50, or the cock which Syawawa provides
to guard his wife in No.16. But it may also be
decorative, like the stringed beads with which
Sinyawi Nyawi adorns his new bride. Sometimes the
provision is not made voluntarily, as in narrative
No.49: the bride does not bedeck her slave with her
own clothes because she wants to, but as forfeit for
the wager she lost earlier.

The second type of Donation - nourishment - also
manifests itself in many forms. The objects which
feature as possible items of nourishment in this
tradition are: *nshima* (Tonga staple diet, thick porridge made from corn flour), meat, cow milk, fellow
animals, wild fruit, maggots, flies, worms, water,
fish, honey, grass, alcohol, human beings, human
milk, and toads. These may be grouped into two categories: those the consumer can procure for himself,
and those that require the intervention of another
party or donor. In the second category, the donor
procures the items of nourishment and feeds them to
the consumer, who functions solely as recipient.
Of the items listed above, fellow animals, wild fruit,
fish, and grass belong to the first category - self-
procured nourishment - because the consumer in this
tradition procures each of them without the assistance of a third party. Fellow animals are obviously
items of a carnivorous diet, while grass is an item
of a vegetarian one; but both are terrestial food
items. Wild fruit on the other hand is aerial while
fish is aquatic. Thus the category of self-procured
food spans the major sources of food supply known to
the Tonga.

Lions are the main eaters of fellow animals, while
human beings rely heavily during periods of famine on
wild fruit, as seen in narrative No.45. Fishing in
the cante-fable tradition, though not in real life,
is often carried out by women, as is evidenced in
narrative No.25, where the girls go to fish by a dam.
(In such instances, however, the fishing grounds are
the abodes of large menacing monster-birds.) Furthermore, what the girls do with the fish seems to be
limited by the cante-fable tradition, since they
usually eat the fish themselves; the tradition seems
to prescribe not only the sex of those who fish but
the sex of the consumers of the fish as well. Grass
on the other hand, is consumed by herbivorous animals
like the zebra in narrative No.61. All items of
nourishment in this category are generally acquired
beyond the frontier of the village, and seem to serve
the sole purpose of enhancing the physical well-being
of those who eat them.

Ordinary food consumed by adult human beings belongs to the category of donor-provided nourishment, because in the cante-fable tradition it is usually acquired by one party (donor) and fed to the consumer. Ordinary food consumed by human adults is generally acquired by an elder kinsman - a father-in-law, as in narrative 34, and fed to a younger kinsman. It may be procured from another village, but is ordinarily consumed within the borders of the consumer's village. When it is not, as in narrative No.34, it portends danger for the consumer. The sole function of ordinary food in this tradition is to sustain the physical well-being of those who eat it.

Maggots, flies, and worms are generally procured by a praeternatural donor and offered to a human recipient. The donor may be an old woman, as in narrative No.43, where the function of the revolting meal is to test the human recipient. If he follows his natural instincts and rejects the meal (like the Hare of narrative No.85), then he never accomplishes his mission. If, on the other hand, he eats the meal (like Fox in the same narrative), he is rewarded with instructions as to how he can accomplish his mission. Water is most often procured by a female donor and given to a male recipient who, as in narrative No.50, later kidnaps her. When a male figure is the donor of the water, the water does not function as an item of nourishment; it portends danger for the recipient. In narrative No.93, for instance, Mazumba is killed by the water his father-in-law offers him. In this tradition, water may be procured and consumed both within and beyond the frontiers of the consumer's village. Honey is usually procured by a male donor and fed to a female recipient. In some instances, however, it is procured by a female donor; but even in those cases the recipient is still a woman. Honey is a food item which is procured solely from the forest and serves only the material well-being of the consumer. The use of alcohol as an item of nourishment is rare in this tradition, occurring only once in the sample. In narrative No.90 where it features, it is procured by an improvident husband for his and his wife's consumption. The result of drinking it excessively is the destruction of the man's family.

Human beings are food for the large monster-birds, as in narrative No.6, or lions, as in No.40. Generally, the predators prey on their human victims in the forest or in the animal village, but in narrative 83 the predators invade the human home and devour its occupants. This deviation from the norm is indicative of some misdeed on the part of the human victims. Ordinarily, the animals eat only the human beings who are foolish enough to wander into the animal habitation or who are brought there by some foolish relatives.

Breast-feeding takes place only between mother and child. By inference, it is the most endearing mode of nourishment in the tradition. Breast-feeding may take place in the home, but it may also take place in the forest, as in narrative No.80, where the young mother breast-feeds her child on the farm. In this tradition it is not only living mothers who breast-feed their children; dead mothers may also feed their living children, as in narrative 79.

From the discussion above of the nature of the nourishment in Tonga cante-fable tradition, one may conclude that in the tradition food serves many purposes; it may, like ordinary food, be for the well-being of the consumers, or it may also function as an indicator of wrongdoing. It may serve as a test for a hero, and it may portend danger for those who eat it. In addition, it is a means of classifying the consumers, for the tradition restricts the kind of food the characters involved are permitted to eat. It is quite possible for animals to assume a human guise; what they cannot do, however, is eat human food like *nshima*. The best method of finding out the real nature of a character in these tales is to examine the kind of food it eats.

Thus there are two major multiforms of donation found in Tonga cante-fable tradition: donation of provision, and donation of nourishment. Although the former deals with items of material culture, while the latter pertains to items of food, both multiforms of the theme involve catering for the physical well-being of the recipient.

Contest

The theme of Contest occurs quite often in Tonga cante-fable tradition and it may involve a test of physical ability, as shown in narrative No.7, where the spirit wrestles with each of the banished twins before adopting them. Each twin throws the spirit and in this way earns the benefits which the spirit later bestows on him. Sometimes the contest is a race in which the contestants try to find out which of them is the faster at running, as in the contest between the Hare and the Tortoise in narrative No.22. In this race, however, the Tortoise changes the contest from a test of physical prowess to one of mental ingenuity, by hiding one of his young ones at various points along the route; hence each time the Hare calls the Tortoise, the young Tortoise ahead of him answers. The Hare imagines that the Tortoise is indeed ahead of him and continues to run until he finally collapses and dies, so that the Tortoise manages to win the contest without even so much as stepping out of his house.

Sometimes the contest is over who shall marry the most beautiful girl in the neighbourhood. Thus, such contests are really tests of physical attractiveness, as illustrated in narratives 26, 20, 48 and 53. In these examples the strong contestants make the first proposals. The smaller ones take their turns only after the stronger ones have failed. Ironically, it is the weakest and thus the least masculine of them who succeeds. In No.26 where the contestants are animal, the Hare marries the beautiful bride. In No.48 where the contestants are human beings, it is a young boy and his companions who succeed in procuring the bride whom their elders wooed without success. A multiform of the marriage contest appears in narrative No.17. Here the contestants are girls, and the contest is to find out which of them will become the bride of the handsome but shy youth, Tembo, who lives in the river. As is usual in such situations, the contestants who appear to be most likely to succeed try first, but they all fail. It is predictably the ugly girl whose body is covered all over with scabs who wins the contest.

A variant of the physical prowess contest is one designed to see which animal is capable of arresting the thief who plunders the communal farm or water-hole, as is shown in narratives 26, 77 and 84. In this form of contest the bigger and stronger members of the community are the first ones to mount guard over the communal property, but it is the smallest member of the community who succeeds in arresting the plunderer.

Sometimes the contest is a test of magical powers, as in narratives 20 and 44. In narrative No.44 the contest is between the son of a man's elder wife and the son of his younger wife over the possession of a magical stick which furnishes its possessor with all the good things of life. As in most contests in this cante-fable tradition, the weaker contestant - the son of the younger wife - paradoxically wins the contest. In narrative No.20 there is a trial of magical strength between an *enfant terrible* and his prospective father-in-law, and the weaker contestant - the prospective son-in-law - wins the contest.

One may therefore conclude that there are various spheres of contest in this cante-fable tradition. Of these, physical prowess, physical beauty, mental prowess, and magical powers seem to be the most important. In all these contests, the weaker contestant invariably triumphs over his stronger opponent.

Attack

Based on the intentions of the attackers, one can classify attacks into four major types. The intention of the first type is to kill or at least to injure the victim, while the objective of the second type of attack is to rescue him. The objective of the third is to kidnap, while that of the fourth type is to rehabilitate the victim.

Most often the reason people attack one another in Tonga cante-fable tradition is to injure or to kill the victim, as is illustrated in episodes in narratives 5, 7, 11, 13, 14, 15, 16, 26, 29, 37, 40, 50, 51, 55, 60, 64, 65, 73, 74, 76, 80, 83, 85, 86, 88, 89, 90, 92, 93, 95, 96, 97 and 99. Sometimes, however, the objective of the attacker is not to inflict bodily injury, but simply to overpower and bring the victim back to his proper home. This is most common in cases of Banished Children and in many such instances, the father of the banished child attacks and brings home his own child. This kind of attack is exemplified in narratives 21 and 46.

There is yet a third kind of attack which is in many ways similar to the second in that it involves the physical overpowering and carrying away of the victim, but differs from it in that the attacker has malicious intentions. The attacker in the third type does not carry his victim to the victim's proper home, but to an alien one. This kind of attack is very common in situations in which someone kidnaps another's wife, as in narratives 11, 50, 57 and 89. As with the theme of Loss, in all these narratives an abductor kidnaps either the wife or daughter of some- one else.

In the fourth type of attack the aggressor inflicts physical injury on his victim, but it is distin- guished from the first type - whose sole objective is to hurt the victim - because there is a desire to rehabilitate him. This is the least common of the four types of attack in the tradition and is repres- ented in narrative No.64, where a father flogs his daughter who carelessly allows his treasured sun to escape into the day.

The narratives do not usually mention the weapons used in the various attacks, but in narrative No.7 the narrator tells her audience that both the attackers and the defenders are armed with guns. Again, in narrative No.64 the narrator informs his audience that the father beats his daughter, presum- ably with a stick.

A study of the result of the attacks in the narra- tives indicates that certain kinds of tales have certain predictable endings. For instance, it appears that the Hare always manages to escape from his attackers regardless of the predicament in which he may find himself, as may be seen from the endings of narratives 5 and 26. But it is not only the narratives about the Hare which have an invariable resolution. When animals marry human brides and later try to eat them, their attacks are invariably

unsuccessful, as may be seen from narratives 40, 55
and 76. Some attacks have limited success. Abductors of women manage to carry away their victims, but
cannot retain them, as in narratives 50, 57 and 89.
Another attack which belongs to this category is that
by the monster Sezimwe, in narrative No.16 he attacks
and swallows Syawawa's wife, but the woman is eventually set free when the monster is killed. The
limited success of the watch dog in narrative No.50
also belongs to this category. It is remarkable that
in each attack the dog kills all the attackers but
one always manages to escape.

One must not imagine, however, that there are no
totally successful attacks in Tonga cante-fable tradition; many attacks succeed completely as narratives
13, 14, 29, 51, 60, 65, 80, 83, 92, 93, 95 and 96
demonstrate.

In a few instances, however, the attack boomerangs
on the attackers, as in narrative No.7, where the
father and his companions, who set out to kill his
wife's imagined lover, are defeated by the defenders.
In many of the narratives in the tradition, however,
attackers who are finally defeated are less fortunate
than the father and his companions in narrative No.7.
In narrative No.37, for instance, the father who
turns into a lion in order to attack and to kill his
son is himself torn to bits by his son's dog, and his
fate is similar to that of the witch in narrative
No.15 who invites some lions to eat her guests, since
they turn on the witch and devour her.

Adoption

The theme of Adoption is often associated with the
theme of Banishment because most adopted children in
the tradition are also children who were earlier banished from their homes. In all the examples in my
collection of tales, the adoptions take place in the
forest and away from the human village. Often the
foster-parents who adopt these youngsters are very
old women who live in the forest, although in narrative No.7 the foster-parent is a spirit with one eye,
one nose, one hand, and one leg. In addition, these
foster-parents are invariably solitary figures; they

have neither spouses nor children of their own.
Furthermore they have no kinship ties with their
adopted children. In some instances (such as narrative No.21) the adoption is only partial because the
foster-parent merely cares for the banished child
while the natural mother continues to provide its
meals. It is the foster-parent who recommends this
arrangement. In other cases the adoption is total,
as is shown in narrative No.56. Here the foster-
parent not only takes care of the baby, but also
feeds her on wild honey which she collects from the
forest. Most often the adoption results from a
mutual agreement between the natural mother of the
child and the foster-parent; but there are instances
where the adoption takes place without the knowledge
or consent of the natural parents, as in narratives 7
and 18.

Throughout my sample, adoption takes place when the
children are very young - usually a few days old -
and lasts till they reach adolescence. In each case
the father who has earlier banished the children welcomes them back home at the end of the period of
adoption. In many cases indeed, it is the reconciliation between father and his banished children which
terminates the children's adoption by the foster-
parent.

Revelation

There are two major types of Revelation of identity
in Tonga cante-fable tradition. The first is the
situation in which someone reveals his own identity,
and the second one in which someone reveals the
identity of another.

The first type, which I call self-revelation, is
more common, and is illustrated in narratives 1, 7,
49, 20, 54 and 90. In narrative No.1, a woman
emerges from the grave and appears to her daughter in
the guise of a bird and reveals her identity to her
daughter. The daughter believes the revelation without hesitation. This is similar to what happens in
narrative No.90, in which a boy does not doubt the
revelation of his mother, now transformed into a
zebra. In narrative No.7, however, when the twins

reveal their identity to their mother, she refuses to
believe them, and only when she looks at them more
closely does she believe that they are indeed her
lost children. Thus, while there is absolute and
undoubting faith in the first two examples, there is
initial doubt in the third.

Sometimes the scepticism is not as temporary as in
No.7. When the new bride in narrative No.49 for
instance, reveals her identity to her new husband,
he refuses to believe that the girl wearing the
tattered clothes is really his bride, while the one
bedecked in fine clothes is his wife's slave. Consequently, he treats the bride as if she were indeed
a slave girl until the bride's parents finally take
her home.

Another instance of refusal to believe a revelation
is narrated in narrative No.54. Here the ghost who
assumes the guise of a human being reveals to the two
girls who want to be his wife that he is indeed a
ghost and cannot marry them. One of the girls
believes him and returns home, but the other does not.
Instead, she follows the ghost to his grave and
stands there till he finally sinks into the earth.

In these examples, the only instances in which the
revelation is believed are in narratives 1 and 90,
where a mother appears in the guise of an animal to
her child. In other instances of self-revelation,
there is either temporary scepticism or total dis-
belief.

In the second type of revelation of identity –
where someone reveals the identity of another to a
third party – the individual whose identity is being
revealed has been cheating the third party, as in
narratives 4, 14 and 42. In No.4 for instance, the
Hare clothed in a lion's skin visits the village of
the Hyenas. Believing that he is indeed the Lion,
the Hyenas welcome him to live in their midst for as
long as he chooses. Each day they go out to hunt for
their guest and while they are away, the Hare casts
off his disguise and dances, meanwhile abusing the
Hyenas for being so gullible. Eventually the young
Hyenas who stay at home hear the Hare's taunts, discover his tricks, and reveal his identity to their
elders. In this and in similar examples in the

tradition it is not in the interest of the exploiter that his real identity be revealed to the third party. This is especially applicable to cases like narrative No.13 and others in which a murderer's identity is revealed.

Sometimes, however, a third party reveals the identity of a character because he is not capable of revealing it himself, as in narrative No.21 and other examples where a girl is banished. In such situations, it is usually someone else who reveals the banished girl's identity to her father.

Thus there are two multiforms of the theme of revelation prevalent in the tradition: self-revelation and third-party revelation. Both deal mainly with the revelation of human identity.

Loss

The Loss of human beings usually entails the loss of beloved relatives, but the tradition strictly limits the possible relationships involved, since the lost person is invariably either a wife or a child. The loss may result from someone adopting the child without the knowledge of the parents, as in narrative No.7, or from some jealous neighbour kidnapping the bride in her husband's absence. Sometimes the loss of a bride is not due to the machinations of outsiders; she may be enticed and abandoned to die on a tree-top by her mother-in-law, as in narrative No.23, or even by her own husband, as in narrative No.96. Sometimes the loss of human beings results from death either from natural causes (as in No.43 where all the ten sons of one woman die one after the other), or from foul-play (as in narrative No.13 where Moonga's friends kill him because he is more successful than they are). The loss of a child eaten by a monster-bird is another variant of the loss of a human being.

Human beings, however, are not the only things that may be lost in this tradition. The loss of treasured objects like the sun, a magical ring, a snake that has healing powers, or a hunting dog may cause great pain to their owners also. The loss may be due to a foolish daughter who lets the sun escape, as in No.64, or a greedy wife who steals her husband's magical

ring, as in No.39. It may be an inadvertent mistake,
as in No.36, where a boy removes the lid from a pot
without realising that it contains a treasured snake.

Thus, the theme of loss deals primarily with the
loss of a beloved kinsman or a treasured object, but
the lost person is invariably either a wife or one's
own child.

Deception

In this tradition, a character may tell a well-
intentioned lie for the sole purpose of furnishing
the questioner with the answer which he would like to
hear (as in narratives 1 and 7). In narrative No.7,
the mother of the twins lies to her husband about the
fate of the banished children and about the source of
the food she brings home from the forest because the
truth would upset him.

Sometimes a character deceives another not because
he fears to hurt his feelings but because he wants to
exploit him, as in No.4 where the Hare exploits the
Hyenas. Exploitation is also the objective of the
deception in narrative No.5. In this, the Female
Hare tricks some nursing animals into pursuing her
until they fall into a trap; thus enabling her to
procure their milk for her own consumption. Narrative No.3 exemplifies an even more brutal form of
exploitation, when the Hare and the Lion deceive the
other animals in order to kill and eat them.

In all these examples of deception the exploiters
are animals. But there are also examples in my
collection where the exploiters are human beings, as
may be seen in narratives No.14 and 42. In No.14 an
old woman feigns illness and deceives her kinsmen by
doing no work. By so doing, she exploits her kinsmen
who toil every day on the farm.

Sometimes the objective of a deception is solely to
inflict injury on others. In these situations, the
victim's suffering does not benefit the deceiver in
any way, as in No.15. Here an old woman - possibly
a witch - who lives in the wilderness, tricks some
girls into spending the night in her home, and then
invites lions to eat them. The girls manage to
escape, however, and the lions turn on the old woman

because they imagine that she has deliberately deceived them. Another multiform of this is narrative No.37, in which a father deceives his son into believing that they are going into the forest to collect wild fruit. But once they reach the forest, the father turns into a lion and tries to kill his son. His son's dog comes to the aid of his master and kills the old man. At other times a man may deceive his wife because he is selfish and wants to keep a supply of food to himself. He hides the food and eats it secretly. The wife usually discovers the husband's trick and retaliates by taking all the food for herself and her children.

In other situations, the purpose of the deception may be to impersonate someone else, as in narratives 28 and 40. The reason for the impersonation varies: in No.28 it is to enable the jealous neighbour to kidnap the Elephant's wife, while in No.40 it is to entice human brides into an animal village so that the disguised lions can eat them whenever they wish. Another objective may be simply to enable an animal bride to get a human husband. In the Igbo cante-fable tradition, such brides later kill their human husbands, but this is not so in Tonga cante-fable, where the animal brides are harmless. In other cases, the purpose of the deception may be to conceal one's crimes (as narratives 13 and 60 demonstrate). Usually the deception does not succeed, and the murderers are exposed. Sometimes the objective may be to destroy the friendship between two people, as in narrative No.78, but this does not achieve its aim. Or it may be simply to cheat a friend (as in narratives 85, 87 and 88). In such situations, the victims generally fare better in the end; so that again the deception does not achieve its desired goal.

Thus the theme of Deception deals with falsehood in inter-personal relations and shows numerous reasons why people deceive one another. In some multiforms, the deceiver's intention is good-natured, but in most it is wicked.

Reassurance

This theme is rare in the tradition. A situation
that calls for Reassurance is one in which someone is
jealous, as is exemplified in narrative No.7, or one
in which two intimate friends are temporarily
estranged as in narrative No.78. Reassurance in such
situations is an attempt to give someone confidence
in his relationship with another.

The reassurance may produce the desired effect, as
in No.78, in which the friends reassure one another
that their association will never falter again. In
narrative No.7, however, the jealous husband remains
suspicious even after his wife assures him that she
does not have another lover.

Jealousy

When a man marries a very beautiful wife, his
neighbours are often jealous of him (as narratives
26, 28, 57 and 89 demonstrate). In such situations,
the neighbours usually try to take away the wife,
either by kidnapping her, as in narratives 28, 57 and
89, or by attempting to kill the husband, as in No.26.
In some instances, such as No.7, it is not the neighbours who are jealous, but the husband who mistakenly
believes that lovers are providing his wife with fine
clothes and delicious meals. Sometimes the jealousy
has nothing to do with a man's wife, but is due to
resentment of a more successful companion, as in
narratives 13, 33, 44 and 92. What the jealous ones
can do is limited; if they are many in number, they
may kill their more successful companion (as in narratives 13 and 92). If there are only two companions
and one of them becomes envious of the achievements
of his friend, the envious one may either go out and
attempt to outdo his companion, or decide to do
nothing at all. In the first case he normally brings
disaster on himself, as in No.43 where a jealous wife
who attempts to revive her dead offspring in the land
of the dead (because her co-wife has successfully
done so), herself dies in the process. Another
multiform of this is No.39, in which a wife is so
jealous of her husband's magical ring that she steals

it. Like the jealous wife in No.43, however, she succeeds only in bringing disaster on herself, because her husband eventually recovers the ring and uses its magical powers to make the wife destitute.

Sometimes the object of the jealousy is intangible, as when it is the friendship between two characters, as in No.78. In this rare situation, the jealous neighbours merely want to upset the friendship between the two companions, but do not hope to benefit from this. Such agents of jealousy without a profit-motive generally fail to achieve even this limited objective of social sabotage.

Thus the theme of Jealousy deals largely with the resentful behaviour of a character's colleagues or spouse. The behaviour may be a reaction to the character's success either in marrying a beautiful wife or in acquiring wealth, or may arise from a husband's resentment of the favours which his wife's lover confers on her.

Doubt

This theme is often linked with the revelation of identity. Very often when the real identity of someone is revealed the third party doubts it. This is the case in narrative No.4 where some young Hyenas tell their parents that the animal pretending to be the Lion is indeed the Hare, but their elders at first doubt the accuracy of the information. Only when they see the Hare shed his Lion's skin and dance in his usual manner do they believe what their young ones told them earlier. Again in narrative No.14, the people on the farm send someone back to find out who is drumming at their home, and when he reports that it is the old woman, the others doubt his story. Only when they see the old woman for themselves do they believe. There are similar episodes in narratives 21, 40, 42, 55, 62 and 76.

But the doubt is not limited to situations involving a third party. Sometimes when someone reveals his identity to another, the recipient of the information doubts the authenticity of the Revelation. This is exemplified in narrative No.7, as I have already shown, where the initial scepticism of the

mother is akin to that of the husband in narrative
No.49, but he continues to doubt the identity of his
real bride to the very end.

Defeat

The situation that invariably leads to Defeat is an
unjustified attack on someone else or a desire to
defraud others of what is rightly theirs. Narrative
No.37 provides the best example of the kind of
behaviour that always results in defeat. Here a
father entices his son to go out with him to look for
wild fruit in the forest. When they arrive, the
unsuspecting youth climbs a tree in order to pluck
some fruit. Meanwhile, his father, who remains at
the foot of the tree, turns into a lion and attempts
to kill his son. The youth manages, however, to
summon his dog, which tears the old man to pieces.
Other examples in which the provocateur is defeated
are narratives 7, 74, 78, 80, 84, 93 and 97.
    The fate of the defeated party varies from one
narrative to another. In narrative No.7, the
defeated father and his companions are invited to a
feast given in their honour, while in narrative No.77
the farmers give the thief, Sikulu Siyamba, a stern
warning, but do not punish him further for stealing
their crops. In No.37, however, death is the fate of
the defeated party.
    Thus, although the situations that invariably lead
to defeat in this tradition are predictable, what
happens to the defeated party is variable and
unpredictable.

Recovery

Death or severe illness are the situations that
create the need for Recovery. In such situations,
recovery usually implies a resurrection from the
dead or recuperation from severe illness, as in narratives 16, 29, 43, 58, 63, 68A, 74, 79, 82, 85, 86
and 99.
    There are two major types of recovery discernible
in this cante-fable tradition. In the first type,
which I shall call kinsmen-induced recovery, the dead

123

person's relatives make his recovery possible. In the second, self-induced recovery, the dead person comes back to life unaided.

There are several forms of kinsmen-induced recovery that one encounters in this tradition. The first occurs through recitation of incantations, as is the case in narrative No.63, but here it appears that the incantation by itself does not suffice. For it to be effective it has to be recited by the youngest member of the family. The second form of kinsmen-induced recovery is due to the overcoming of the charm that holds the dead captive. This applies especially to situations involving ritual rather than physical death, as in narrative No.58. Here a boy is ritually dead because his parents have already given him a funeral, but he is not really dead; his mother's jealous co-wife merely holds him captive, entombed in a gourd. His father and mother bring about his recovery by breaking the power of the charm which has held him captive. In another multiform of the kinsmen-induced recovery, the relatives simply visit the abode of the dead and take them back to the land of the living. This mode of recovery seems to apply only when death is due to natural causes (as narratives 43, 68A and 79 illustrate). It is remarkable that in the land of the dead - terrestial in No.43 but aquatic in narratives 68A and 79 - those who die a natural death lead lives akin to those of normal living people. For this category of dead people, recovery may call for the performance of sacrificial rites, as in narrative No.79, where a husband sacrifices a cow to the river after he has recovered his dead wife from it. Yet another mode of kinsmen-induced recovery is by the dismemberment of the monster that has swallowed the dead, liberating the victims. This is the manner in which the wife of Syawawa is rescued in narrative No.16, and the same mode of recovery is found in narrative No.29. Kinsmen-induced recovery may also be brought about by the intervention of a herbalist, but this seems to be effective only for those seriously ill and not for the dead.

Instances of self-induced recovery, which entails someone raising himself from the dead, are rare in this tradition. There are instances in which someone has fainted but is not really dead, as may be seen in narrative No.46, where a father who faints later comes back to life. The only instances of genuine resurrection from the dead involve animals and not human beings, as in narrative No.99. Here some rats which the hunters kill revive themselves even after they have been salted and dried in the sun. Other instances are found in narratives 41, 71 and 117. It may be concluded that genuine cases of human self-induced resurrection are hard to find in Tonga cantefable tradition.

Recognition

The theme of Recognition often involves the Return of someone who has been away for a period of time. The two are distinct themes, however, because they do not always occur together. Recognition is an important issue during the first meeting of the returned one with someone at home.

The reason for the absence from home may be due to a variety of reasons, such as a long Banishment or even death. The visit of a dead person to his living kinsmen is a situation that usually calls for recognition. The tradition limits the number of possible guises in which the visitor from the land of the dead can appear. It may be in the guise of a bird, as in narratives 1, 60 and 92, or as he was before he died, as in narratives 68A and 79. The tradition limits the options open to the visiting dead even further; both men and women can return in the guise of a bird, but only dead women have the option of appearing to their kinsmen as they were before they died. When the visitor from the land of the dead appears in the guise of a soul-bird, the living relatives invariably do not recognize him; hence, the visitor always has to reveal his (or her) identity. On the other hand, when the visitor appears like her former self the relative recognizes her instantly.

The purpose of such visits is again limited by the tradition. If the visitor appears as a soul-bird, his purpose may be either to expose his murderers to his kinsmen (as in narrative No.60 and 92) or to

125

assist the kinsmen in some other way, as in narrative
No.1. But if the visitor appears as her former self,
her purpose must be to render assistance to the
living kinsmen. She cannot appear in this manner to
accuse her murderers.

Apart from the visitations by someone from the land
of the dead, there are other situations which involve
the theme of recognition. One such situation is
generated by a father's visit to the forest home of
his banished child as in narratives 7, 18, 21 and 56.
Another situation is the one in which certain jealous
people kidnap someone's wife or daughter. As mentioned in the discussion of the theme of Loss, the
woman's protector usually searches for his kidnapped
ward and finds her in the abductor's village, as in
narratives 11, 19, 50, 57, 75 and 89. Invariably the
husband recognizes his wife as soon as he sees her
even in situations like the one in narrative No.75
where her abductors disguise her. Another situation
where recognition is necessary is one where someone
who comes home uses a song as a secret code to
instruct those at home to let him in. Invariably,
the code falls into enemy hands: perhaps those of
hostile neighbours who use the code to kidnap the
person inside the house, as in narrative No.28. But
the enemy may be a lion, which kills the persons who
let him into the house, as in narrative No.83.

Sometimes the recognition arises from a woman's
search for her child who was adopted without her knowledge, as in narrative No.7, or who is dead, as in
narrative No.43. It is ironic that in such situations the woman generally recognizes her long-dead
children when she sees them in the land of the dead,
yet when a mother sees her twin sons who have merely
been lost, she is unable to recognize them. Sometimes a man marries a wife from a distant land. In
real life, his representative would chaperon the
bride on her first journey to the home of the husband,
but in the cante-fable tradition a bride may be
accompanied only by her slave girl. The arrival of
such a bride and her slave girl at the home of the
bridegroom creates a situation in which recognition
of the bride is essential to the development of the
narrative. The bridegroom in this unusual situation

126

invariably fails to recognize which of the two girls is his real bride and which is the slave girl. Without exception he mistakes the slave girl for the bride and treats his bride as if she were the slave girl, as in narrative No.49. It is not only husbands who are unable to recognize their kinsmen; parents too in certain circumstances fail to recognize their children. One such situation arises in narrative No.20. Here, a day-old boy sets out to procure a bride for himself and when he brings home the bride, his parents do not recognize him until he reveals his identity. Again, in narrative No.70 the young boy who guards his father's farm becomes so emaciated that when he returns home, his parents fail to recognize him till he reveals his identity to them.

Thus the theme of Recognition is found typically in situations where two kinsmen meet after a long period of separation. The returner usually recognizes the kinsman he left behind earlier, but most often the relative at home does not recognize his long-departed kinsman.

CHAPTER VI

Themes of Reintegration

This chapter deals with the third category of themes, which in the present sample is represented by only four: Return, Reception, Reconciliation, and Reintegration. Thus they constitute half the number of themes in the first category and about a quarter of those in the second. They belong together because within the framework of the tale of the Banished Child, which is our point of departure, all of them take place when the parents and their banished children return home from the forest dwelling.

Return

In some narratives that deal with the theme of Return, the principal character or hero simply comes home and the story ends; nothing else happens to him. In many other narratives, however, a variety of events follow. Sometimes when the hero comes home, his kinsmen prepare a great feast for him, and this serves as a rite of Reincorporation, which reintegrates the hero into the community from which he set out earlier to achieve his fame, as in narrative No.52. The return of Banished Children is another situation which usually calls for such reincorporative feasts, as narrative No.7 demonstrates. There are other ways, however, in which returning heroes may be reintegrated into the society. In narrative No.21 there is no feasting when the heroine returns; her father merely welcomes her back and then formally rescinds his initial prohibition tabooing her birth. This is the situation also in narrative No.100, where the formal rescinding of the taboo has an element of a rite of reintegration, because it formally removes the barrier that separated the tabooed girl from the rest of the community. Sometimes the incorporation of the returning hero is limited to the villagers' gathering and welcoming the hero back from his arduous journey, as in narrative No.25.

In this tradition a wife has a choice of two places

to which she can return if she is the heroine of the
narrative, either to her husband's home or to the
home of her parents. When a wife exercises her second option and returns to her native home rather
than her marital one, it is usually a sign that something is wrong with her marriage, as in narrative
No.29 where a wife decides to return to her parents
after fighting with her husband. A hero's return
home may be a prelude to yet another journey, for the
hero may find on his return that his dear one has
been kidnapped (as in narrative No.50) and has to
journey to the village of the abductors in order to
rescue his kidnapped kinsmen.

Sometimes he returns home to find himself heir to a
large fortune, but more often the wealth is produced
by a magical object - a ring, a stick, or a small
pot - given to the hero while he was on his journey
(as in narrative No.52). There may be no public
celebration of his return; his parents are simply
overjoyed to see him and spend their time telling the
hero how much they missed him while he was away.
This is what happens in narrative No.58, where the
parents, imagining that their son is dead, had given
him a funeral. When they finally release him from
the charm holding him captive, they spend the night
telling him how much they missed him.

Sometimes the hero does not return in the manner in
which he set out; he may be killed on the way by his
companions, usually because he is more successful
than they. Although the murderers usually conceal
their crime, either the hero's pet animal - as in
No.13 - or the hero himself in the guise of a soul-
bird - as in No.92 - returns home to condemn them.
In such situations, the dead hero's kinsmen usually
put the murderers to death. There is only one
example - No.87 - in my sample of tales where the
travellers who return without their companion escape
this fate, and here it is the river which has drowned
her for stealing communal fruit.

In one instance - No.83 - a heroine meets her death
when she returns home, but this is not retribution
for someone she has murdered, as is the case in No.13;
it is simply the fate of wayward girls. In another
multi-form where death follows the return of the hero,

it is not the hero who dies, but the hero and the cannibal wife whom he marries who bring death to all the members of his family. The hero learns from his bride how to devour human beings and when they have eaten all the members of the hero's family, they turn on the wife's family too.

Thus, the theme deals primarily with the Return of the principal character or hero to the community from which he earlier set out to achieve his fame.

Reintegration

When someone has been away from home for a long time, his return usually calls for his Reintegration into the society from which he has been away. The tradition, however, limits this special treatment to the principal character or hero of a narrative only. This explains why the normal husband's absence from home at the birth of his unwanted children, frequent in Tonga cante-fable tradition, does not occasion any reintegration, since the husbands are usually not the heroes of such narratives.

The long absence which calls for reintegration may be occasioned by a variety of causes, often by the hero's banishment from his home in early childhood. As mentioned earlier such absence from home tends to last from early infancy to Adolescence. This is the case in narratives 7, 18, 21 and 56. Sometimes, however, the absence may be caused by the enchantment and captivity of the hero by his mother's co-wife, as in the case in narrative No.58. At other times it may be due to the hero's quest for a wife, which may last from early childhood to early adulthood, as in No.20. Or the absence may be caused by a heroine's sojourn in the world of her animal husband.

Reintegration in this tradition is invariably a rite of passage which helps the one returning to adjust to his or her role as a member of the society from which he or she has been away for a long time. It also gives the community an opportunity to welcome the hero or heroine back into its fold.

Reconciliation

The prior estrangement of close relatives or
friends is a situation that calls for Reconciliation
in the cante-fable tradition. Since the notion of
close relatives in Tonga society embraces not only
one's nuclear family but one's entire matrilineage
as well, it is theoretically possible for estranged
persons to comprise a young boy and his matrilineal
uncle. (A young man traditionally inherits the
property of his matrilineal uncle rather than that of
his own father; hence a matrilineal uncle is a close
relative). But the tradition strictly limits the
kinsmen who can be estranged, and it must consist of
either a father and his twin sons, as in narrative
No.7; or, more often, a father and his daughter, as
in narratives 21 and 56. In the cante-fable tradition, a mother is hardly ever estranged from her son
or from her natural daughters, but the estranged pair
can be a man and his wife. As was mentioned earlier,
the estranged persons need not be members of one
family; they can be merely friends, as in narrative
No.78. But this is not as common as the situation
that involves members of the same family.

The duration of the estrangement varies from one
narrative to another. In No.35, for example, we are
not even told how long husband and wife were apart.
In narratives 7, 21 and 56 the estrangement lasts
almost from the very birth of the children to the end
of their adolescence. In No.78, however, it lasts a
much shorter time.

Every instance of estrangement between members of
one family in my collection represents basic marital
disharmony; hence, the eventual reconciliation of
such estranged persons removes the discord in the
family. This applies equally to the situations that
entail the estrangement of intimate friends. Furthermore, in the cases that involve father and children,
the Reconciliation paves the way for the ultimate
reintegration of the Banished Children into their
native village.

Reception

Receptions in this tradition are formal gatherings
involving many people. There are numerous occasions
that may call for a reception; it may be a prince's
wedding, as in narrative No.1, or the unexpected
arrival of a father and his companions at the forest
home of his Banished Children, as in narrative No.7.
Sometimes, however, the occasion for a reception may
be the return of a daughter who was banished, as in
narrative No.21, or who has been living with a new
husband who later transformed himself into an animal,
as in narrative No.81. The occasion may even be the
recovery of an elder kinsman from a severe illness.
Thus one may conclude that although there are a
variety of situations that may call for a reception
in the cante-fable tradition, all of them are happy
ones, as in real life.

Feasting is a common aspect of the receptions.
Usually the narrator does not describe the details of
the feast, but in some narratives one learns the
names of the snimals slaughtered for it. In narrative No.21, for instance, a father slaughters several
heads of cattle for the reception which he gives in
honour of his daughter; so that one may deduce that
the feast is fairly elaborate.

******

This discussion of the nature of the three categories of themes found in the tale of the Banished Child
shows the kind of thematic materials the narrators in
this tradition use in their rapid compositions before
their traditional audiences.

A narrator who is experienced in the tradition has
usually listened to numerous narratives in which
various multiforms of the themes which comprise the
tales that are known to him are present. As a result,
he has learnt from experience that certain themes
make certain kinds of tale resolution possible. He
may not know all the multiforms of even the themes
which he uses in his own composition; such knowledge
is not necessary. Again, he usually does not have a

132

metalanguage wherein to discuss his themes. Nevertheless, he is usually aware of the options which the
themes he uses make possible: he knows for instance
that the birth of twins always leads to the banishment of children. Consequently, such an experienced
narrator generally tends to recreate the traditional
tale resolution in his own process of composition.

CHAPTER VII

Thematic Comparisons

Having demonstrated the existence of themes in the Tonga tradition of cante-fable, it is now necessary to break down these multiforms of the tale of the Banished Child into their constituent themes, with a view to discovering the degree to which the tales resemble one another.

Narrative No.7 will again be the starting point, and the themes will be numbered serially in the order in which they occur in the narrative. The numbers on the left hand margin indicate the sequential order of the incidents in each multiform, while the ones on the right indicate the thematic sequence. Each time a new theme appears, it will receive a number on the right hand margin and will be represented by that number each time it recurs in the entire narrative. In this way narrative No.7 may be represented as follows:

1	Marriage	1
2	Enumeration of spouses	1A
3	Conception	2
4	Enumeration of Conception	2A
5	Birth	3
6	Enumeration of Birth	3A
7	Elaboration of Birth	3B
8	Repudiation	4
9	Protest	5
10	Banishment	6
11	Journey	7
12	Donation of Provision	8
13	Elaboration of Donation	8A
14	Further elaboration	8B
15	7	
16	Deception	9
17	Transformation	10
18	Application of Donation	8C
19	Neglect	11
20	Adolescence	12
21	Adoption	13

66	Attack	27
67	Defeat	28
68	24	
69	18	
70	22A	
71	Reconciliation	29
72	7	
73	Reintegration	30

Thus narrative No.7 comprises seventy-three episodes, but utilizes only thirty different themes. Hence the ratio of incidence to theme is about 5:2.

I shall now attempt to break down narrative No.6, performed by Agnes Nagn'andu, into its constituent themes in order to find out the degree of similarity between them and the themes of narrative No.7. When I encounter a theme in narrative No.6 which is identical with a theme in narrative No.7, I shall assign it the same number as the theme in No.7. If I find a theme in narrative No.6 which does not exist in No.7, however, I shall assign the new theme a new number. On this basis the themes in narrative No.6 may be represented as follows:

1	1	
2	1A	
3	3B	
4	3B	
5	6B	
6	7	
8	4	
9	22	
10	7	
11	Donation Sought	8D
12	7	
13	16	
14	Murder	1OA
15	22	
16	Instruction Rejected	22A
17	7	
18	Bird's consumption of Woman's Children	1OA

Here there are eighteen incidences and nine different themes; hence, the ratio of incidence to theme is
exactly 2:1. In addition, all the themes in this
tale also occur in narrative No.7, which is approximately four times as long as narrative No.6. On the
basis of the great affinity between the themes in
narratives 6 and 7, one is justified in classifying
them as belonging to one cante-fable family.

Turning to narrative No.46, I shall attempt to
break it down into its component themes in the same
way:

1	1		
2	1A		
3	2		
4	2A		
5	Prohibition of birth of girl	6A	
6	3		
7	3A		
8	3B		
9	7		
10	8		
11	9		
12	12		
13	8C		
14	12		
15	2		
16	3		
17	7		
18	8		
19	7		
20	21		
21	23		
22	21		
23	9		
24	24		
25	21		
26	19		
27	18		
28	Temporary Death	1OB	
29	Recovery	31	
30	6B		
31	29		

137

Here there are thirty-one incidences and sixteen distinct themes; hence the ratio of incidence to theme is about 2:1. Thus the ratio of incidence to theme in narrative 46 is about the same as the ratio of incidence to theme in narrative No.6. Furthermore, of the sixteen themes that occur in narrative No.46, only one is absent in the two preceding tales. Hence, one may conclude that the thematic contents of narratives 6, 7 and 46 are sufficiently similar to warrant classifying the three narratives as belonging to one cante-fable family.

Applying the principle devised in the analysis of the three preceding tales on narrative No.21, its thematic contents can be represented as follows:

1	1	
2	1A	
3	6A	
4	2	
5	2A	
6	3C	
7	3D	
8	7	
9	13	
10	22	
11	8C	
12	12	
13	Purification (Rainfall)	21
14	21A	
15	7	
16	23	
17	18A	
18	7	
19	18	
20	7	
21	23	
22	18	
23	27	
24	23	
25	30	
26	Elaboration of Reintegration	30A

Here there are twenty-six incidences and fourteen
themes resulting in a ratio of incidence of theme of
almost 2:1 - the ratio in narratives 6 and 46. There
are no new themes which were not present in the other
narratives already examined. Since all the themes
that compose narrative No.21 are found in the three
preceding tales, narrative No.21 definitely belongs
to the same family of cante-fables as narratives Nos.
7, 6, and 46.

If one applies the analytical model above to narrative No.56, one finds that its thematic content may
be represented as follows:

1	1
2	1A
3	3C
4	3D
5	8
6	8C
7	8C
8	12
9	7
10	27A
11	7
12	18A
13	7
14	27A
15	7
16	18A
17	7
18	27A
19	7
20	30A

Here there are twenty incidences and eight distinct
themes, resulting in a ratio of incidence to theme of
approximately 5:2. It is remarkable that here, too,
all the themes that compose the tale are the ones
that have already been encountered in narratives 6, 7,
46 and 21. This proves conclusively that narrative
56 belongs to the same cante-fable family as narratives 7, 6, 46 and 21.

If one applies the analytical model above to narrative No.100 the following thematic scheme results:

1	1
2	1A
3	2
4	6A
5	3D
6	3C
7	8
8	8C
9	12
10	12
11	7
12	27A
13	18A
14	18B
15	18C
16	7
17	9
18	7
19	7
20	18A
21	7
22	27A
23	7
24	30A

Here there are twenty-four incidences and eleven
distinct themes, resulting in an incidence to theme
ratio of about 2:1. It is noticeable too that all
the themes that constitute narrative 100 are found in
the narratives which have already been examined.
Hence, narrative No.100 undoubtedly belongs to one
cante-fable family as narratives No.7, 6, 46, 21 and
56.

Narrative 18 is of special interest because it was
performed by the mother of Scholastica Mutinta - the
narrator of No.7. Although Scholastica said that she
had learnt the cante-fable from her mother, her
version of it (as is seen in narrative No.7) was
longer and more developed than her mother's. This
reveals the real nature of the process by which the
oral narrative is transmitted from one generation to
the other. It is often assumed - though not always
stated explicitly - that the person from whom one
learns a story is a better performer of that

particular tale than his student. This may be true
when the student is a novice, but does not apply when
the student has acquired a mastery of the tradition,
as is clearly seen by comparing Scholastica's telling
of the story of the Banished Child with her mother's.

Comparing these two multiforms of the tale of the
Banished Child supports Lord's contention that talented narrators or singers of tales do not merely
recite what they have memorized but that each performance by a talented narrator is indeed a creative
composition.[10] If the narrator merely recited what
they had memorized then narrative Nos.7 and 18 would
be identical. The great difference between the two,
however, proves convincingly that narrators use the
stories they have learnt merely as a framework around
which to build their own compositions. Hence, the
difference between two narrators' multiforms of the
same story is not determined solely by the difference
in the learned multiforms.

When one applies the analytical model above to the
thematic contents of narrative No.18, the following
scheme results:

1	2
2	2B
3	3B
4	4
5	1
6	5
7	8A
8	13
9	8
10	22
11	7
12	4
13	8C
14	12
15	13
16	17
17	7
18	20
19	7
20	23
21	8C

22	7
23	7A
24	31
25	8D
26	7
27	27
28	5
29	7
30	7A
31	7
32	6B

Here, too, there are fourteen distinct themes and thirty-two incidences; hence the ratio of incidence to theme is about 5:2 - the same ratio as in narratives 7 and 56. All the fourteen themes which comprise this tale are found in the six preceding tales.

To summarize, the analysis above shows that the thematic contents of each of the seven tales of the Banished Child resemble one another so closely that the seven narratives are undoubtedly multiforms of one another.

CONCLUSION

The study has revealed that there are two major
levels of compositional organization in the Tonga
tradition of cante-fable: the thematic and linear
levels of organization. The thematic organization
concerns the nature of the themes, while the linear
organization deals with the manner in which the
themes and the various units of the narrative combine
with each other. These levels of composition are
circumscribed by the tradition because the boundaries of each theme are defined by the tradition. In
the same manner, multiforms of a narrative generally
have a pattern of occurrence of the major episodes.
For instance, in the tale of the Banished Child, the
birth of the unwanted child usually precedes the
banishment of such a child. Again, the banishment of
the unwanted offspring generally precedes the reconciliation of parent and child that ultimately culminates in the reintegration of the banished offspring
into his father's community. Furthermore, the
enactment of a Tonga cante-fable normally entails a
linear progression from the introductory piece to the
signature.

What the study demonstrates is that every narrative
in the Tonga tradition of cante-fable is defined by
the habits of thematic and linear composition that
are permissible within the tradition. These habits
must not be viewed, however, as iron-clad barriers
that inhibit a narrator's creative talent. It has
been shown by detailed analysis that each theme has
numerous multiforms. This, in turn, shows that the
tradition allows a narrator ample choice of narrative
material. What these organizational practices do is
define the parameters of traditional composition.
Within these defined boundaries a narrator is at
liberty to exercise his creative talents to their
utmost.

From all indications, it appears that the Tonga
tradition of cante-fable, as well as other genres of
Zambian oral literature, is declining, due to several
factors. Principal among them is the ban which the
early Christian missionaries placed on such practices.

Secondly, the rapid intrusion of the transistor radio
has changed the entertainment habits of these people.
As a result, many Tonga nowadays turn to the radio
sets for entertainment rather than to the narrative
sessions, as was the case in the past. Besides,
since Zambia is one of the most highly urbanised
African countries, it means that a large percentage
of the rural folk have migrated to the urban centres,
which are certainly not ideal settings for the growth
of the tradition of cante-fable.

Aware of this decline, the government of independent Zambia is trying to revive the tradition by
incorporating it into the school curriculum. It is,
however, too early yet to assess the impact of this
governmental intervention.

APPENDIX I

Narrative No.7
Conteur: Scholastica Mutinta
Copy Reel No.1

Mbukaniinga #*
Kwaali musankwa #
Waatwele Maali #
Bakaintu hobile aba #
Baatumbiki(a) antoomwe #
Unw(i) (w)aazyala mwana omwe #
Ono awa umw(i) (w) aazyala babili #
Waboola mwanalumi #
Inino ndikoona buti nubakaintu?
Ono ebe ozyala bana bobile #
Nsyekuyanda pe #
Ndikoona muli moomu
  muli mwana omwe #
(I) no mbocicitwa musa #
Kut(i) ime nsyikwe kucikon(zy)a kayi koona
  bana boon(a) akati.
  Ino me katoona lili andiwe ndikoona boobu #
Ma! (i)n(o) oyo musankwa #
Tacinjili mula ba syinamaanga aba #
(I) no (w) alo woona buyo mili mukaintu omo
  ujisi nwana omwe #
Mwaali #
Ono ati (w) ebo baama
  nsyekuyandi ncobeni ulandisofwazyizya
  (a)lubwa #
Kobweza bana aba ukabasowe #
Kufumbwa nkoyanda (a)mbweni ukabatule kwenu #
Ma! wasinizya omulu maangu? Uti kasimpe #
Wakayumuka mukaintu oyo #
Ibula bwa nwana #
Ono mbasowe bana bangu baneneede ncobeni
  bulowa mbukwako. Uti ndamanizya biya,
  syita koyanda kuti nze kubajaye kolanga #

---

*Throughout the text the audience's response
'Kalangati' will be represented by this symbol.

Wakayumuka mukaintu oyo #
Wakusika mucisaka #
Azyi kucebuke so #
(W)ajana kuli makobel(a) aamulonga #
Amane nkuyanda ceembe (w)aatole(le) zya ceembe #
Nku(g)wama zyitebi zyakaindi zya muumba #
Ino waumputa akwa, waumputa #
(I)cimw(i) (w)acita cakulya #
(I)cimw(i) (w)acita payi #
Wabasyonka muniini munkomwe yabbwe #
Wabalazyika bana #
(I)no (w)apilukila kumaanda #
(I)no waakubasowa mwinangu bako bana?
   Uti ndabasowa, mfwilwe buyo ng'anda #
Ndalumba, mbwenjanda obo.
   Kay(i) on(o) oyu nacikomezya nwana nsyeona kabotu #
A! (N)kobal(i) oko #
Bwaca biyo cifumo-fumo wafuma #
Bwaca biyo #
Kumazuba cifumo-fumo kumazuba #
Cimwi ciindi nicaasika ciindi cakukomena.
   bana liva ni bamikila so #
Ha! uti ndabakomezya basankwa bangu.
   Baali basankwa balo #
Ino obo buzuba #
Bakacelwa cifumo-fumo ati ma! (mbo)ndakasiya
   zyakulya mbobalya sunu ndaunka kumazuba #
Kuboola nkaga syikuulu kumwi #
Ino kayi nobasankwa bangu nywebo nwihilayi?
Kuti mpamp(a) awa ano biya mpaa ng'anda yokwesu #
A! A! mpaa ng'anda yokwenu kunyina abanyoko? #
Nkuti bataata nkobali. Ino pesyi ndaliluba zyina lya
   kutusanina #
(I)no mebo ndali kuyanda kuti nobasankwa bangu
   mupe mulimo kakuligwasya mbomunyinina uso #
(I)no inga tobana-bana ulatugwasya buti? #
(A)ti kamuboola kuno kumusenga #
Lweendo koboola #
(Ndi)tinge #
Kadidilika kana kadidilika kana du #
(Wawa syik)uulu kumwi #
Kobool(a) ayebo Mpimpa #
Waunka Mpimpa didili didili du #
Ha! Mwacilya coolwe nobasankwa bangu #

146

Kamuboola #
Ino kayi twaunka baama bahikulijaya #
Uti tabalijayi kamuboola biyo baya kulila mbuli
  bwaaka lumbula uso #
Batolana #
Mbaakabatola leelyo #
(I)nsondo yaakumana #
(I)no bamane banyina baboola nibaaleta zyakulya #
Batiti kulang-langa #
Kwasyaala zyiteba #
Batiti kulanga-langa #
Wabajaya bakomena kale bana bangu.
  S yena mulum(i) (w)angu waka ndeena? #
Waunka mutumbu kumesyo nkuya bulila #
Waunka uya bulila. Akasike kumaanda oko #
Ma! Tungungu #
(I)no kayi sunu musa unyema-nyema nzi? #
Nkuti nee, moyo wangu inga mpaawo yabingila
  ndayeeya bana bangu #
Uyeeya bana bako bakaboola
  kaindi akuboola abayeeyegwa nzi? #
Nkuti nee musa syii bakaboola.
Kayi # tufumbwa
  wakafuwa lili ngoo takzyiba wamu yeeya
  mapenzi, wayeeya kuti sunu basanyina
  mbaoaya nebali boobu #
Alo myoyo ya zyikaintu biya #
K(o) umuna biyo musa #
A! Yamana nsondo #
Alimwi inkainzile #
Akeende so kuya kusika kuti #
Ma! waile kwiima mutumbu so #
Kwaka yaka mukuw(a) aakali bana bangu? #
Mawee! #
Inga batiti(i) ino nibaka yaka,
  bacita luwaile ino kuli biyo igeeti #
Balisukata Syena uli mukuwa okakala abana bangu? #
Wazwa kale Lweendo # Ikuti ndiswe baama #
Ndiswe baniini biya. Kamuboola kamuzya buyo
  mwiimikile awa Ndendiswe sikuulu kumwi
  nguwaa tutolede #
Wakaa kutupa zyoonse zyibelesyo mbuli
  mukuwa muta yoowi. Kwaamba ndize mundijaye teesyi?
  nkuti ndendiswe #

147

Bakaima geeti. Mbabana bangu #
Bamunjizya mucembele mung'anda Yalila nguluulu
   mizinga. Nkuti mutalijayi #
Impenzi lyamana #
Taata kumbele amazuba uya kuba nweenzu kuno #
Ndinywe biya ndinywe? Nkuti a kaulu komwe,
   a lisyo lyomwe a nkoye yomwe #
Twakali kuya ku bihigwa ngu wakaakutu komezya aboobu#
Akaka Leza aa ndigwasye, nobana bangu amulange
   mbindaba maulu #
Balaamba kuli Mpimpa, banjizye mu bbahwa baama
   oko Mpimpa #
Waba sanzya #
Waba sanzya #
Waba sanzya bazyuumpa zyisani ezyi #
Baba samika amabbusu #
A nsipa #
Baba nanika kabotu kabotu, baba samika #
Bamane kwayandigwa disyi pati biya disyi #
Nkuti ono baama ezyi nzyotuti bike moomu
   mutani (k)ya kumwiimi taata pe #
Nkaàambo nokuli kuti atusowe swe mizimo
   nkwiili kusyute yakwe #
Ono kasimpe syuwa mukabe anguwe, muka seke seke
   mutakanyeme #
Olo atumine zyili buti ulafwa iwakwe #
Alimwi mutali kuya ku danduli kamwiile kumwine
   biyo kuti mujana ku mukow(a) anu #
Ndalumba taata, bakamba-kamba bacembele #
Babika zyoonse zya makuwa nzyimuzyi kale zyiligwa
   zyoonse babwezu baba twika #
Batalika ino baya kweenda, baba sindikila a ntobolo #
   (Lwiimbo)
                    Yaa kuwa ko Syimutema-Mbalo
                    Ku munzi Nyanga zumina
                    Yaa kuwa
                    Mawee!
                    Yaa kuwa koo loobwe
                    Taata mba ka kaka maanga
                    Zyuumbwe zyini a kasowe
                    Yaa kuwaa
                    Mawee!
                    Yaa kuwa koo loobwe
                    Yaa kuwa ko syimutema-Mbalo

                    Ku munzi Nyanga zumina
                    Yaa kuwa
                    Mawee!
                    Yaa kuwa koo loobwe

Baama, no bacembele, ngaalya maanda kamuya ino #
Nkweenda mutumbu, nkweenda #
Akasike, nkuti konditula, usyi ndaba #
A! wakuweza nzi mwin(a) angu #
Nkuti bataata bakali kunini oku ku mukuwa baka
    ulisyizye ng'ombe. Ino ati mukalye
Langa mwatalika kukoka. Wakamba. Wakamba
    mutumbu mucembele oyo mulumi wakamba #
Nku njizya mung'anda #
Inga ncaati pasule mudaala #
Ma! Ma! Ma! Ma! Inga ncatiti peepe #
Kucinyina ati mutacili kulya nsima buya
    tu pime nsondo imane mutani kulya nsima.
    Nkulya bubodo bwalo. Batalika Nkuumpa tii,
    zyoonse ba etelwa sintu inketulo, tukapu
    toonse, Ino kojatila kooku mulam(a)
    angu tuli bakaindi uta zyijayi #
A! O mwin(a) angu, nsikwe kusoomona?
    Kuti nceciyandika lizwe dooti lya nsima ya
    kaindi #
Lino katulya bukuwa #
Tuneneye biya #
Ino balo balila mubana bakaboola. Izona (a)
    (wa)kaamba kuti bana bakaboola. Bamupazyezya
    ino katulya. Nee, ati taata waamba kuti
    mbo bana bako bakafwa mukalye a mulum(i)
    ako ndakajaya ng'ombe. Njakulila ba
    mwana eyi ng'ombe i ulwazyeezi
    Eena musa #
Bana bakaboola. I bakaboola Kulya #
Kulya #
Alimwi (w)aunka biyo, weenda mutumbu weenda #
Mbwaa pompela uti baboola kale bacembele
    Koyamika ntobolo. Zya ima laini
    ati ndiza kuli uba sinkikila
Batalika baboola kubacinga #

                    Yaa kuwa ko syimutema-mbalo
                    Ku munzi nyanga zumina

                              149

Yaa kuwa
Mawee!
Yaa muwa koo loobwe
Taata mbakakaka maanga
Zyuumbwe zyini a kasowe
Yaa kuwa
Mawee!
Yaa kuwa kuwa lo loobwe

Konjila mucembele, konjila.   Meenda akapya kaindi #
Katutana Kwaanzya koya kasembe.
  Kobagusya zyisani bacembele #
Bawacilwa banjila zyimbi #
Babambwa bahambwa babambwa.   Ino mbuba kali
  Kukala aceya #
Nku baiisya cilinanikwa eeci citubya kumeso.
  kamucite boobu #
Ambi oyo.   Nkuti peepe biya nobana bangu uso #
Sunu masiku abulo walikundaambila kuti
  kuti ukazyeete sunu nkutand(a) akaya,
  alimwi nzinini zyalo mung'aanda
  Nsyaandi kala nunka #
Me ndati pe.   Utabindi kutanda nee ndiza
  mebo yamana ng'omb(e) eyi ndakala biyo #
In(o) oyo ulaa nwana onwe.   Ino mebo ning'ombe
  biyo icili azya kulya zyili boobu #
Ati nee!   Koya biyo ndikwiile kuumpa nwin(a)
  angu koya #
Weenda #
Oko nkwali mutumbu ulabambwa nkwali #
Ba!   Injende ulandizukula taata #
Ani munsi watyani?   Nee, munsi ono watamba #
Ati ndakatazyigwa zya kulya ezyi, zyiboola buti? #
Imwana wakafwa (ka)taka lilwa mpoona
  alimwi (kuk)afwe ng'ombe? #
Kamubweza zyoonse ntobolo #
Oyu mukaintu wangu, wakatwalwa mukuwa #
  Ma!   Nkweenda buy(o) oko mwana a musimbi
  baya bwiimba:

                Yaa kuwa ko syimute-mbalo
                Ku munzi nyang zumina
                Yaa kuwa
                Mawee!

                        150

Yaa kuwa lo loobwe
Taata mbakakaka maanga
Zyuumbwe zyini a kasowe
Yaa kuwa
Mawee!
Yaa kuwa koo loobwe

Mpimpa langa baama kwasiya kofwambaana #
A! Beenda #
Baamu Kamu alimwi baama kamweenda kabotu,
  mazuba ta(kwe) kuvula taata ulatubona #
Nkaambo wa(ka)tupa swe oyo wakatupa bwami obu
  abungan'anga bwa kubona bazya #
Ono kamweenda kabotu mutali ku bbodooli,
  kamwiile ku umuna kabotu kabotu #
Wa pompa kale. Mawee! Mawee! Mawee!
  Wakweta kale limbi tiba #
Ino nkujan(a) atusani-sani twa mudaala
  wakubikilwa awalo usyi #
Musa katulyanzyeezyi zya kulva.
  Waakucela kale mwin(a) angu? Nkuti inzya #
Ma! al mwi yeba mwin(a) angu kutinta cenjeli
  ndanyangwa #
Nkuti tonyangwi nee. Kayi kuzyalwa syita
  yeb(o) otayandi bana. Meebo taata ula
  ndiyanda maningi #
Ma! Balya Balya #
Kwasiya. Ono musa ezyi zyisani kaka zyilaa
  dooti, mi inga ndoona kayi ii (nsyi) boni
  kabotu njina #
Yebo sama zyeezyi, amapayi aya atwaaleke #
Ma! Banjila #
Bacite boone #
Nkuya ku mukaintu musyoonto #
Nkuti baama na ulaa kwenu akusowa mwana
  usowa biyo ciindi #
Mbo bulumbu bwako #
Koile kuya kwanu buya.
  Cifumo njane mung anda waka, wakata.
Nsye kuyanda. Ono inga ndakala buti koya
  kanjile moo ndaba muya #
Mula katazya. Bona mwan(a) amusimbi taaumununka
  nsipa. Nsye ciyandi biya dooti #
Acu! I o kayi niba toona biina ndaba niba

151

ndaambila mbuba kaa kucite mwana
bana babo we! #
Nkuti ooyu ndakaamba kuti kasowe,
muciindi ca(ku)ti ndaacili ku kuyanda,
kasowe bana me tutwalan(e) anduwe #
Ono w(e) a nyama yoonse ati bweele langa #
Nsye ciyandi biya a dooti ulaa dooti
koya biya kwenu pilukila limwi. Waile
kukamba mukaintu #
Ba! Nkoona #
Bucic(a) awalo ku pakinga oko masik(a) ati
ulandijaya #
Nkweenda #
Buciya kuca mwanalumi oyo #
Kuya kusondela nkujana bakaintu bakaunka #
Mboobu mbondali kuyanda #
Ino ono musa uciknozye kukal(a) andime
mbondaajaya bana ndiza zyeelo zyika
ndi boolele? #
Nkuti nee! nku(ku)paulwa mane O! Usyilikwe.
Peepe #
Ono mukaintu nkweenda wa yumuka #
Ino uya kale ku nkuni? Nkuti inzya musa,
njakusikilizya akwesu #
Ino awalo #
Nkweenda #
Musankwa #
Nkuya kwanbila baabo mbaa katamba syintobolo #
Nkuti ono zuba lyacita boobu mpayanda kuboolela #
Ono nywebo?
Ndakaliko kweena #
Uli waawa, uli waawa oyo mukuwa umutwele.
Ono anywebo muka zinguluke mukacite so
mu luwaile ntobolo #
Bakamane cilili biy(a) abya bantu baamukwata
bakamane cilili tu kakale mumo a mukaintu
wangu #
Walo atakafwi pe #
Ma! Ino awo #
Wakusika kale mwana a musimbi
            Yaa kuwa ko syimutema-mbalo
            Ku munzi nyanga zumina
            Yaa kuwaa
            Mawee!

Yaa kuwa ko loobwe
Taata mbakakaka maanga
Zyuumbwe zyini a kasowe
Yaa kuwaa
Mawee!
Yaa kuwa ko loobe

Bababona kale bacembele babatambula #
Ikut(i) ino nibwakaa kuti licenguluke zuba
  ba bambwe bacembele #
Ya komka a kukomoka nkamu #
Nkwiili kuti ka! A! Nobeenzuma #
Twafwa Lweendo! Sanzya twafwa! Nkuti Iwedi.
  kofwambaana biyo ko eta ntobolo izya cifwefwe #
Bazwa. Nkuti mtabindi biyo kuti mamuli basyi
  kujaya #
Swebo tula mumanizya #
Inga kuya kuzyitondeka, boonse ansi wukukamba #
(I)no nibakamana booba basankw(a) abo nibakawa
  ba syikujaya #
Bakabuka akuba, kuba cita boonse mu lubuwa ba
  banjizya #
Nkokuleta zya kulya zyoonse zya kulya #
Zyoonse zyoonse zya kulya kuti imulye #
Iswebo ndendiswe baama twaka sowelwe. webo taata #
Ndendiwe taata. Swe baama katuya tukutondezye
  motwaka komenana #
Ono mutabi aneo mucita cinji cinji. Zyoonse nzyo
  mupengele ka mwaamba biyo tumupe #
Babuka bantu abo batambilwe kufubazya mudaala:
  uyanda kiyiza bana bako, langa yebo
  wakupuka waba mukuwa #
Niuti kwiina ncindaazyi basa #
Ono amundigwasye biyo batakaki mbatole
  ku munzi nkabajaile ng'ombe bakasotoko.
  Mebo njanda kuti ndelwe kuli mbabo.
  Milandu ndiilila kuli mbabo #
Nko kudweema mudaala oyo. Bana bakwe wakabatola #
Syii bakaimba kaimbo pe #
Bakasike kumbo a munzi #
Yajaigwa ng'ombe. Bii sotoka, bii bika mu
  mootokala, yaazyi kufundilwa kuli mbabo #
Nga mamanino aakaano ako #

Ndamana. Ndime Scholastica Mutinta, Muka Mwami Moonze.

APPENDIX II

Once upon a time #*
There was a young man
Who had two wives. #
Having married two wives #
The two women #
Gave birth at the same time #
One gave birth to one child #
The other one gave birth to twins #
When the husband came home #
How shall I sleep #
My wives #
Now you have twins #
I do not love you any more #
I will sleep in the house where there is only
  one child #
Is this the way it should be done? #
I will not be able to sleep, if the children
  sleep in the middle (of the bed) #
How can I sleep with you, sleeping like this? #
So the young man #
Stopped going into the house where the twins lived #
He slept in the house where the wife had only
  one child #
Now the truth is that I do not love you.
  You will bring dirt into my compound. #
Take these children and throw them away #
Take them wherever you want. You can take
  them to the home of your parents if you want #
Have you made up your mind, my husband? Is this
  truly what you want? #
The woman set out #
With the children #
Now I must throw my fat children away. Your
  own blood #
I have nothing else to say except you want me
  to stand up and kill them while you look on #

---

*Throughout the translated text, the audience's res-
ponse 'kalangati' will be represented by this symbol.

The woman set out #
She went into a forest #
When she looked back #
She saw a river and reeds growing on its bank #
Then she looked for an axe #
She had taken an axe with her. She cut some
  old branches #
Now she began to beat the bark of the tree. She
  beat it #
She spread one (on the ground) #
She improvised a blanket with the other #
She hid the twins in a cave among the rocks #
She made the children comfortable #
Now she went back home #
Have you thrown away the children, my wife? She said
  I have thrown them away because
  I do not want you to divorce me #
Thank you. That is what I want #
While the other (wife) raises her child,
  I shall sleep well #
In your house #
Time passed #
Very early in the morning she got up #
To go and feed her twins #
After a while the children learnt to stand up #
She rejoiced, saying I have raised my young
  boys. They were boys #
One day #
She was late in the morning. She said to herself
  since I left them food and they can feed
  themselves I will go in the afternoon #
Then came a one-legged spirit #
He lives in the forest and is rare to see #
He came without delay and stood on the rocks #
Now my young boys, where do you come from? #
If you mean here, this is our home #
Ha! Ha! This is your home...
  without your mother? #
My father is nearby, only I have forgotten
  his name and the name of my mother. No ·
  we live here. When we grow up
  each man will take care of himself. But
  our mother comes to do what, to feed us #

Now I want to give you a job so that you can
    help yourself, as you have no father #
How can you help us, since we are very
    young? #
Come here to the sand #
Lweendo, come here #
Wrestle with me #
The boy staggered. The boy staggered
    Kadidilika kana, kadidilika kana du #
The one-legged spirit fell down #
Come here also, Mpimpa. He staggered
    didili, didili du #
You are very lucky, my boys #
Come here #
If we go, our mother will kill herself #
She will not kill herself. Come. She will
    cry just as she had done when your father
    drove you away #
They went #
He took them #
One week went by #
The mother brought some food #
She looked everywhere #
She saw only the barks of the tree #
He has killed my children who are already big.
    Did my husband deceive me? #
The woman went away, crying #
She went away crying. When she reached home #
She was depressed #
Why are you so depressed today, my friend? #
No my heart sometimes aches when I think of my
    children #
You are thinking of your children who are rotten
    already. Why do you think of them anyway? #
No, my friend, they are not rotten. Whenever you
    think of those who died and you did not
    know them well... It is a shame when you
    realise that had they lived, they would
    be the same age as those living #
Womens' hearts! #
Keep quiet, my dear #
Ah! One week went by #
Let me go and search again #
She went and when she arrived #

She stood there #
A rich man has built a house where my children
   used to live? #
Mawee! #
When he built the house he even constructed a wire
   fence around it... and a gate too #
She braced herself. Are you the rich man
   living with my children? #
Lweendo had already come out #
It is us, mother #
We are the little ones. Come and stand here. It
   is us. The one-legged spirit who took us #
He gave us all the tools, just like a rich man.
   Why are you afraid? Perhaps you
   will kill me, thinking that I am not the
   one? It is us #
They stood at the gate. These are my children! #
They took the old woman into the house. You
   must not kill yourself #
My troubles are over #
In future you will have a visitor here #
Truly, you are the one? Because of the
   one who has one leg, one eye, one eye-lash #
He is the one who brought us up #
God help me. Look at my feet #
He said to Mpimpa 'take our mother to the
   bathroom' #
They bathed her. They bathed her. They bathed
   her and they burnt her clothes #
They made her wear a pair of shoes #
With soap #
They annointed her well and they
   clothed her #
Afterwards they looked for a large container #
Now what we shall put into the container,
   you must share with our father #
Although he threw us away, we bear his name.
   Truly, surely, stay with him. You
   must smile. Do not be angry #
In spite of whatever he may do, he will
   also die #
You must not boast. Be quiet and say that
   your father gave these things to you #

157

Thank you very much, the old woman said as
    she clapped her hands (in appreciation) #
They gave her every delicious food
    you can think of. They lifted them
    and helped her carry the presents.
    They began to walk. They escorted
    her and they carried their guns #

            Yaa! It has fallen in the outside world
            In the village of Nyanga Zumina
            Yaa! It has fallen
            Mawee!
            Yaa! It has fallen at Loobwe
            The father rejected the twins
            Their graves he will throw away
            Yaa! It has fallen
            Mawee!
            Yaa! It has fallen at Loobwe. ˙
            Yaa! It has fallen in the outside world
            In the village of Nyanga Zumina
            Yaa! It has fallen
            Mawee!
            Yaa! It has fallen at Loobwe.

Mother, our old woman, see the houses. Go now #
The woman went on #
When she arrived, she said help me set the
    luggage down, father-of-someone #
Ah! What did you bring home my wife? #
My father went to town..... he sold a cow.
He said we must eat because we are becoming
    thin. The husband clapped his hands in appreciation#
He took the things from the container #
Ma! Ma! Ma! Ma! Oh no #
Now we shall not eat *nshima**. We shall eat rich
    men's food. They began by making tea.
    They had everything they needed, like
    a kettle and cups. Hold it here my
    husband. We are old people. Do not
    break them #
Ah! my wife, will these things not upset my
    stomach? Perhaps what we need do is

Nshima, thick maize porridge, is the staple food of
    the Tonga people.

158

throw away the dirty, old nshima #
From now on, we shall eat only rich men's food #
We shall become fat. #
But they were mourning the children who were
   rotten. She did not tell him the truth #
No, my father gave me these presents in order
   to console me because of the death of my children.
   He said that I must eat them with my husband. He
   slaughtered expensive cattle in order to mourn my
   children. So that is it, my dear. The children
   are rotten? They are rotten. Eat #
Eat #
The following day, the woman went to visit her
   twin sons. She walked and walked. As soon
   as they saw her from a distance one said
   'the old woman has come, take down your
   gun.' They formed a line, fearing that
   somebody might have accompanied her #
They went out to meet her #

>   Yaa! It has fallen in the outside world
>   In the village of Nyanga Zumina
>   Yaa! It has fallen
>   Mawee!
>   Yaa! It has fallen at Loobwe
>   The father rejected the twins
>   Their graves he will throw away
>   Yaa! It has fallen
>   Mawee!
>   Yaa! It has fallen at Loobwe
>   Yaa! It has fallen in the outside world
>   In the village of Nyanga Zumina
>   Yaa! It has fallen
>   Mawee!
>   Yaa! It has fallen at Loobwe.

Come in, dear old woman. Come in. The water was
   warm already #
Before we welcome you, go and take a bath.
   Remove her clothes #
They washed the clothes #
They washed the clothes and she wore other clothes #
Then they entertained her lavishly.

When she sat down, she felt uncomfortable.
  They taught her how to use skin
  lightening cream. You should
  apply it like this #
Ambi! Ambi! This is Ambi (cream).
  No, no, no, my children. Your father #
  said to me last night, 'If you bring home more
  presents, I will expel my other wife
  since there are too many flies in her house.
  I do not want her. She stinks.' #
I said no you must not be in a hurry to drive
  away the other wife because this cow
  will not last for ever #
Your other wife has one child, but I have
  only a cow which yields food in this
  manner #
No just go. Meanwhile I shall make the tea,
  my wife. Go #
She went #
There they looked after her very well #
Oh! I must go lest my husband finds out #
But the husband had followed her. He was
  curious. I am troubled about this food.
  How does it come? #
The child died and was not mourned and
  now a cow died? #
My wife has another lover #
The child-of-a-woman was on her way and she sang:

      Yaa! It has fallen in the outside world
      In the village of Nyanga Zumina
      Yaa! It has fallen
      Mawee!
      Yaa! It has fallen at Loobwe
      The father rejected the twins
      Their graves he will throw away
      Yaa! It has fallen
      Mawee!
      Yaa! It has fallen at Loobwe
      Yaa! It has fallen in the outside world
      In the village of Nyanga Zumina
      Yaa! It has fallen
      Mawee!
      Yaa! It has fallen at Loobwe.

Mpimpa look here, it is getting dark. Hurry #
Have a good journey. There are so many
  that our father may see us #
Because the one who gave us.... the one who
  gave us the riches gave us the power
  to see what will happen in the future #
Now go well. Do not be proud. Be humble #
Now she is back home. Mawe! Mawe! Mawe!
  she has brought another large basin #
This time with a few clothes for the old man #
My dear, here is the food. Let us eat.
  You have brought food already? Yes #
My wife, if I am not careful someone will
  take you away from me #
No. Nobody will take me away from you. I was
  born... but you do not like children.
  My father loves me very much #
They ate and ate #
Now my dear, your clothes are dirty. When I
  sleep I almost always see lice crawling
  on them #
Wear this and let us not use these blankets
  any more #
They went in #
When they were about to go to bed #
The man went to the younger wife #
My dear, even if you could find somewhere to
  throw away your child, you would still
  be wasting your time #
This is my present to you #
Go back to your parents. When I wake up
  tomorrow morning, I want to see your
  house already locked #
I do not love you. Why should you stay? Go and
  look at the other house #
You are very troublesome. Look at the child-of-a-
  woman. Only soap smells in her house.
  I do not want dirt any more #
Ah! if only she were not already asleep, she
  would tell me how she disposed of her
  children #

161

I told her to throw them away, but I still
  loved her. Go and throw your
  children away so that we may continue
  to be married #
But in your case, even an animal can see it #
I do not like dirt. You are dirty. Go home
  permanently. The woman clapped her
  hands (in submission) #
They slept #
When it was dawn she packed her things,
  fearing that her husband might kill her #
She went away #
When it was dawn the husband went to check her
  house and found that she had already
  gone away #
This is what I wanted #
Now will you want to live with me? I killed the
  children. Perhaps the evil spirits may
  come #
No. Oh! you want to be treated? No. Now the
  woman set out for the forest again #
Are you going to fetch firewood? Yes, my dear,
  I will go as far as my parents' home #
He also left the house #
The man? The man #
He went to tell his friends who had guns.....
  the ones he had invited before #
When the sun goes like this, that is when she
  returns #
But you #
I am tired of being cheated #
He is there..... the rich man who is her lover.
  Encircle the house and do like this on
  the wire fence with your guns. Her
  lovers must be wiped out. They must be
  wiped out. I shall live there with my wife #
She must not die #
Then #
The child-of-a-woman arrived.

          Yaa! It has fallen in the outside world
          In the village of Nyanga Zumina
          Yaa! It has fallen
          Mawee!

                Yaa! It has fallen at Loobwe
                The father rejected the twins
                Their graves he will throw away
                Yaa! It has fallen
                Mawee!
                Yaa! It has fallen at Loobwe
                Yaa! It has fallen in the outside world
                In the village of Nyanga Zumina
                Yaa! It has fallen
                Mawee!
                Yaa! It has fallen at Loobwe.

They saw the old woman and they went to meet her #
But when the sun turned and they wanted to bathe her#
The comb broke #
They said a! my friends #
We are in trouble..... the journey..... bathe.....
   we are in trouble..... get ready..... hurry.....
   bring the fast guns #
They came out. Hurry! If you want to die, we
   shall kill you all #
When the twins took aim, their father and his
   companions fell down, clapping their hands #
Finally their father and all his companions
   surrendered #
The twins got up and invited all of them into
   their home #
They brought food #
Eat everything #
We were the ones who were thrown away. And you #
You are our father. Let us go and show
   you where we grew up #
Do not worry. Tell us whatever you need and
   we shall give it to you #
The old man's companions began to mock him. You
   wanted to kill your children. Look, now you
   have become a rich man. You have become
   a very rich man #
I did not know anything, my dear friends #
Now please help me to persuade them to return
   to the village so that I may slaughter
   cattle in their honour.....so that we may
   all rejoice. I want them to take care
   of me. I am begging them to forgive me.#

Then the old man stood up and took his
   children home. They did not sing any song #
When they reached the western end of the village #
   they skinned it #
This is the end of the story #

I have finished, I am Scholastica Mutinta,
   wife of Mwami* Moonze.

* Mwami is the honorific title of a Chief.

NOTES

1 Brian Fagan, ed., *A Short History of Zambia*
 (Nairobi: Oxford University Press, 1966),
 pp. 88-92.

2 Elizabeth Colson, 'The Plateau Tonga of Northern
 Rhodesia,' in *Seven Tribes of British Central
 Africa*, eds. Elizabeth Colson and Max Gluckman.
 (Manchester: Manchester University Press, 1961),
 p.133.

3 Claude Levi-Strauss, 'Structural Study of Myth,'
 in *Reader in Comparative Religion*, eds. William
 Lessa, and Evon Vogt. (New York: Harper and
 Row, 1972), pp. 289-302.

4 Arnold van Gennep, *Rites of Passage*, trans.
 M. Vizedom and G. Caffee. (Chicago: Chicago
 University Press, 1972).

5 J. Torrend, *Specimens of Bantu Folk-Lore from
 Northern Rhodesia* (London: Keegan Paul, 1921),
 p.3.

6 Ruth Finnegan, *Oral Literature in Africa* (Oxford:
 Clarendon Press, 1970), p.385.

7 Torrend, *op. cit.*

8 Torrend, *op. cit.*, p.6.

9 David E. Bynum, A Taxonomy of Oral Narrative Song;
 The Isolation and Description of Invariables in
 Servocroatian Tradition. (Unpublished Ph.D.
 Thesis. Harvard University, 1964), p.39.

10 Albert Lord, *Singer of Tales* (Cambridge,
 Massachusetts: Harvard University Press, 1964),
 p.4.

11 Van Gennep, *op. cit.*

12 Bynum, *op. cit.*, pp. 119-120.

SELECTED BIBLIOGRAPHY

Abrahamsson, Hans. *The Origin of Death; Studies in African Mythology*. Uppsala: Almquist and Wiksell, 1951.

Allan, W., Max Gluckman, D.U. Peters, and C.G. Trapnell. *Land Holding and Land Usage among the Plateau Tonga of Mazabuka District*. Rhodes-Livingstone Museum Occasional paper, 14, Livingstone, Zambia, 1945.

Anderson, W.H. *On the Trail of Livingstone*. Mountain View, California: Pacific Press, 1919.

Arnaud, Marthe. 'Mythologie et Folklore sur le Haute-Zambeze,' Presence Africaine, 11 (1948), 244-66.

Babalola, S.A. *The Content and Form of Yorouba Ijala*. Oxford: Clarendon Press, 1966.

Bascom, W.R. and Kerskovits, M.J., eds. *Continuity and Change in African Cultures*. Chicago University Press, 1958.

Bascom, W.R. 'Folklore Research in Africa,' JAF, 77 (1964), 12-31.

Beidelman, T.O. 'Hyena and Rabbit': A Kaguru Representation of Matrilineal Relations, *Africa*, 31 (1961), 61-74.

Beier, H. Ulli, ed. *African Poetry*. Cambridge: Cambridge University Press, 1966.

Bick, C. 'Chikuni Mission and its People,' *Zambezi Mission Record*, VII, 107 (1925), 452-4.

Bleek, W.H. and L.C. Lloyd, eds. *Specimens of Bushman Folklore*. London: George Allen, 1911

Buchan, David. *The Ballad and the Folk*. London: Routledge and Keegan Paul, 1972.

Burton, William F.P. *The Magic Drum, Tales from Central Africa*. London: Methuen, 1961.

Burton, William F.P. 'Oral Literature in Lubaland,' *African Studies*, 2 (1943), 93-96.

Bynum, David E. A Taxonomy of Oral Narrative Song; The Isolation and Description of Invariables in Serbocroatian Tradition. Unpublished Ph.D Thesis, Harvard University, 1964.

Casset, A. 'The Chikuni Mission,' *Zambezi Mission Record*, V, 49 (1910), 92-5.

Casset, A. 'Funeral Customs among the Batonga,' *Zambezi Mission Record*, V, 74 (1916), 407-8.

Casset, A. 'How the Batonga were saved from Starvation,' *Zambezi Mission Record*, V, 76 (1916), 465-9.

Casset, A. 'St. Mary's Out Station, Chikuni,' *Zambezi Mission Record*, VI, 82 (1918), 101-3.

Casset, A. 'Some Batonga Customs,' *Zambezi Mission Record*, VI, 86 (1919), 207-11.

Chadwick, H.M. and N.K. *The Growth of Literature*. 3 vols. Cambridge: Cambridge University Press, 1932-40.

Cipriani, L. 'The Anthropological Investigation of the Batonga of Northern Rhodesia,' *South African Journal of Science*, XXVI, 541-6.

Clark, J. Desmond. 'A Note on the Pre-Bantu Inhabitants of Northern Rhodesia and Nyasaland,' *Northern Rhodesia Journal*, 2 (1950), 42-52.

Colson, Elizabeth. *Marriage and the Family among the Plateau Tonga of Northern Rhodesia*. Manchester: Manchester University Press, 1958.

Colson, Elizabeth. 'The Plateau Tonga of Northern Rhodesia,' in Elizabeth Colson and Max Gluckman, Eds., *Seven Tribes of British Central Africa*, Manchester: Manchester University Press, 1961.

Colson, Elizabeth. *The Plateau Tonga of Northern Rhodesia*. Manchester: Manchester University Press, 1962.

Colson, Elizabeth. 'Modern Political Organization of the Plateau Tonga,' *Africa*, XVIII (1948), 272-83.

Colson, Elizabeth. 'Possible Repercussions of the Right to Make Wills Upon the Plateau Tonga of Northern Rhodesia,' *Journal of African Administration*, 11 (1950), 24-35.

Colson, Elizabeth. 'A Note on Tonga and Ndebele,' *Northern Rhodesia Journal*, 11, 35-41.

Colson, Elizabeth. 'Role of Cattle among the Plateau Tonga,' *Human Problems in British Central Africa, Rhodes-Livingstone Journal*, XII (1951), 10-46.

Colson, Elizabeth. 'Shortage of Implements,' *Human Problems in British Central Africa, Rhodes-Livingstone Journal* XIV (1954), 37-8.

Dorson, Richard M. ed *African Folklore*. Bloomington: Indiana University Press, 1972.

Douglas, Mary. *Purity and Danger*. London, Routledge and Keegan Paul, 1966.

Douglas, Mary, and Phyllis Kaberry, eds. *Man in Africa*. London: Tavistock Publications, 1969.

Dundes, Alan, ed. *The Study of Folklore*. Englewood
    Cliffs, New Jersey: Prentice Hall, 1965.

Engels, F. 'Records of Missionary Travel in South
    Africa,' *Zambezi Mission Record*. 1, 5 (1899),
    160-1.

Evans-Pritchard, E.E. *The Zande Trickster*. Oxford:
    Clarendon Press, 1967.

Fell, J.R. *Ingane Zya Batonga e Zimpangaloko Zimwi.
    Folk Tales of the Batonga and Other Sayings*.
    London: Holburn, n.d.

Finnegan, Ruth. *Oral Literature in Africa*. Oxford:
    Clarendon Press, 1970.

Forde, Cyril Daryl. *African Worlds; Studies in
    Cosmological Ideas and Social Values of African
    Peoples*. London: Oxford University Press, 1954.

Georges, R.A., ed. *Studies in Mythology*. Homewood:
    Illinois, Dorsey Press, 1968.

Gluckman, Max. *Custom and Conflict in Africa*.
    Glencoe: Illinois, Free Press, 1955.

Harding, C. *In Remotest Barotseland*. London: Hurst
    and Blackett, 1905.

Hemans, Mrs. H.N. 'A Short Account of the Customs of
    the Bashankwe and Batonka Tribes, together with
    Notes on the Migration of the Barotse from
    Victoria, Southern Rhodesia,' *Proceedings of
    Rhodesian Scientific Association*, XVI (1918),
    5-9.

Herskovits, Melville Jean. 'The Study of African
    Oral Art,' JAF, 74 (1961), 451-456.

Hole, Marshall. 'Notes on the Batonga and the
    Batshukulumbwi Tribes,' *Proceedings of Rhodesian
    Scientific Association*, V, Pt II, 62-7.

Hood, Mantle. *The Ethnomusicologist.* New York:
McGraw Hill, 1971.

Hopgood, C.R. 'Conceptions of God among the Tonga of
Northern Rhodesia,' in E.W. Smith, ed., African
Ideas of God. London: Edinburgh House Press,
1950.

Jaspan, M. *The Ila-Tonga Peoples of Northwestern
Rhodesia Ethnographic Survey of Africa: West
Central Africa,* Pt. IV. London: International
African Institute, 1953.

Jones, A.M. *African Music.* Rhodes-Livingstone Museum
Occasional Paper, 2. Livingstone, Zambia, 1943.

Jones, A.M. *African Music in Northern Rhodesia and
Some Other Places.* Rhodes-Livingstone Museum
Occasional Paper, 4, Livingstone, Zambia, 1949.

Levi-Strauss, Claude. *The Raw and the Cooked.* trans.
John and Doreen Weightman. New York: Harper
and Row, 1970.

Levi-Strauss, Claude. 'Structural Study of Myth,'
William Lessa, and Evon Vogt, eds. *Reader in
Comparative Religion.* New York: Harper and Row,
1972, 289-302.

Livingstone, David. *Missionary Travels and
Researches in South Africa.* London: Murray,
1857.

Livingstone, David. *Narrative of an Expedition to
the Zambezi and its Tributaries.* London:
Murray, 1865.

Lord, Albert. *The Singer of Tales.* Cambridge,
Massachusetts: Harvard University Press, 1964.

Moreau, J. 'A Letter from Monze,' *Zambezi Mission
Record,* III 33 (1906), 93-4.

Propp, Vladimir. *Morphology of the Folktale.* trans.,
    Laurence Scott. Bloomington, Indiana: Research
    Center in Language Sciences, 1968.

Radin, Paul. *The Trickster: A Study in North
    American Indian Mythology.* New York:
    Philosophical Library, 1956.

Read, J.G. *Report on Famine Relief: Gwembe, 1932.*
    Livingstone, Zambia: Government Printer, 1932.

Reynolds, Barrie. *The Material Culture of the People
    of the Gwembe Valley.* Manchester: Manchester
    University Press, 1968.

Seligman, Charles Gabriel. *Races of Africa.*
    London: T. Butterworth, 1930.

Smith, Edwin W., and A. Dale. *The Ila-Speaking
    Peoples of Northern Rhodesia.* 2 Vols. London:
    Macmillan, 1920.

Smith, Edwin W., and A. Dale. 'Addendum to the Ila-
    Speaking Peoples of Northern Rhodesia,' African
    Studies, VIII (1949), 1-9, 53-61.

Syaamusonde, J., and P. Shilling. *Naakoyo Waamba
    Caano Cakwe (Old Naakoyo Tells Her Story) with
    Monze Mukulu (The Great Chief).* Ndola, Zambia:
    Africa Literature Committee, 1947.

Thompson, Stith. *Motif-Index of Folk-Literature.*
    6 vols. Helsinki: Folklore Fellows Communica-
    tions, 106-109, 116, 117, 1932-6.

Thompson, Stith, and Aarne, Anti. *Types of the Folk-
    Tale.* Helsinki: Folklore Fellows Communica-
    tions, 184, 1961.

Thompson, Stith. *The Folktale.* New York: Holt,
    Rinehart, and Winston, 1946.

Torrend, J. *Specimens of Bantu Folk-Lore from
    Northern Rhodesia.* London: Keegan Paul, 1921.

171

Turner, Victor. *Schism and Continuity in an African Society: a Study of Ndembu Village Life.* Manchester: Manchester University Press, 1957.

Turner, Victor. *The Ritual Process.* Chicago: Aldine Press, 1969.

Turner, Victor. *The Forest of Symbols.* Ithaca: Cornell University Press, 1970.

Van Gennep, Arnold. *Rites of Passage.* trans. M. Vizedom and G. Caffee. Chicago: Chicago University Press, 1972.

Werner, Alice. *Myths and Legends of the Bantu.* London: G.G. Harrap, 1933.